MAP *of* SHADOWS

A MAPWALKER NOVEL

J.F. PENN

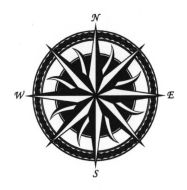

Map of Shadows. A Mapwalker Novel Book 1
Copyright © J.F.Penn (2017). All rights reserved.

www.JFPenn.com

ISBN: 978-1-912105-83-0

Requests to publish work from this book should be sent to:
joanna@CurlUpPress.com

Cover and Interior Design: JD Smith Design
Printed by CreateSpace

CURL UP
PRESS

www.CurlUpPress.com

"It is not drawn on any map; true places never are."

Herman Melville, Moby Dick

PROLOGUE

MICHAEL FARREN SAT AT his desk in the old map shop, an antique parchment in front of him portraying the ancient city of Bath. An oversize globe sat on a low table nearby, its sepia tint displaying a seventeenth-century world that no longer existed. The borders had moved, the names of the countries had changed, and yet he kept it here to remind himself of what had once been. And what could be again.

His shop sat on Elizabeth Buildings, around the corner from The Circus, a circle of power built around one of the porous gates into the Borderlands. By day, he sold vintage maps to visiting tourists. By night, he watched and waited, performing the etching ritual. His gnarled hand held the fountain pen he had used for a lifetime of cartography as he traced over the fading lines on the map with a fine nib.

But tonight, Michael's hand shook as he etched the lines he knew so well with ink of blood and pitch. He tried to concentrate on the arc of the Royal Crescent, the straight line of Brock Street and the curves of The Circus. They were symbols of ancient Druids, a crescent moon attached to the sun by a narrow ley line, a power running deep under the earth.

The Circus was modeled on Stonehenge, the outer circumference matching the temple of Druidic power not far from here on Salisbury Plain. The Mapwalkers had protected the border for so long, but now, something was coming. It had been building in strength, biding its time, waiting until the Ministry was weak. Now there were only a few pure blood Mapwalkers left, and the Shadow Cartographers were rising.

The clock struck one and the cry of a night bird came from outside Michael's open window. The air smelled of summer, elderflower and honeysuckle … But then, something else.

Sulfur.

The air crackled, and the wind picked up, blowing into the shop. The maps on the walls lifted, their rustling sound speaking of change and borders redrawn.

"No, no," Michael whispered as he traced the lines faster, trying to restore the integrity of the carefully planned city. But his pen slipped as the ink began to rise off the page, a thick black ooze that obscured the precise Georgian streets. In the mirror of its shine, Michael saw the shapes of Borderland creatures, teeth bared as they slunk through the trees. The map began to change, the streets of Bath shifting as darkness crept into squares and gardens.

He reached for the phone, pressing a key code he'd only used once before back in darker days he had hoped never to see again.

"It's weakening," he said to the Ministry official who answered. "I'm going to perform the ritual. Send Bridget as soon as you can, but I'll get started. There's no time to wait."

Ignoring the protests on the other end of the line, Michael hung up. He grabbed his leather satchel and walked out of the door into the little pedestrianized street. Clouds scudded across the night sky above him, and a sudden freezing wind whipped his coat around his legs, blustering down between the buildings.

A howl rose up, a feral sound of wild creatures with no

place in this city. Michael quickened his pace, almost jogging to the end of the street, past the art gallery and left towards The Circus, only meters away.

A dense fog, a mist of undulating grey, obscured the circle of tall plane trees in the center of the Georgian terrace. The street-lamps flickered as Michael walked into the round, taking a breath as he tried to see within.

Thunder rolled overhead, and a flash of lightning lit up the sky, arching over the mist as it began to rain. There were shapes within the fog, slinking bodies with sharp teeth, pacing at the edges of the grey as it pushed out away from the inner circle.

Michael's heart raced. It had been a long time since he had faced Borderland creatures, since he had drawn this hard on his blood magic. He had hoped that the sacrifice of his family line was done with and that watching and renewing the lines would be enough. But now, the edges of the Earth-side map were blurring, and if they were to protect the city of Bath and this version of the world, then he had to go in there. It was one level of magic to etch lines on a map, but another to etch them into the earth itself.

He took a step towards the mist, clutching his leather satchel tight against his chest, the instruments of the Cartographer inside. He opened the flap and pulled his antique five-pointed compass from within. It was silver in a turned ivory pocket case, made in the seventeenth century, a time of explorers when the Cartographers were powerful men who carved up the earth, drawing the borders that would shape the political landscape. This compass had been present at the division of the Borderlands when his ancestors had shored up the boundary lines. Its needle had pointed to true north since that day.

Now Michael looked down as the needle spun around, wildly oscillating back and forth, unable to discern the right heading. He tucked it inside his waistcoat pocket, taking another step forward, steeling himself to enter the haze.

Tendrils of mist curled out towards him, wrapping around his feet, a subtle pressure, probing, testing. A chill ran through his bones and Michael gasped at its touch. He sensed the influence of a Shadow Cartographer here, one of those who sought to redraw the boundary and open the porous border to the feral horde beyond. He had to get to the center of the circle before it was too late.

Michael stepped into the mist, and the city of Bath receded, the curved terrace buildings disappearing as he walked further in. The circle of trees was only a few meters across, but it was as if he stepped into a forest. The heavy trunks loomed over him, leaves dripping with rain as it pelted down from above. The air was thick, and Michael's breathing became labored as he struggled to inhale the viscous atmosphere. It stank of the Borderlands beyond, a fetid soup of the diseased and dying, rotting flesh and the rubbish of those clustered in the camps without hope. So unlike the pristine civilization of Bath that he and the Ministry lived to protect.

A howl came from further in, echoed by another, calls from the wild wolves that had once roamed this land. They had been driven into the Borderlands, hunted to the edge of extinction like so many of the species in the realm beyond, waiting for their opportunity to roam free again. But they did not belong here, and he would not allow them to run loose in his city.

Michael caught a glimpse of one behind a tree, its powerful body still as it stared at him with yellow eyes. It growled, baring its teeth. The sound sent a shiver up Michael's spine, the call of the predator triggering ancient fear inside. But this was his realm, even though they were pushing at the boundary. He still held power here.

He pulled a ritual knife from his satchel, the yellowing ivory blade bound with a leather strap, tied into a series of knots around the end. Passed down from the time of the Druids, the blade had been used to sacrifice for many moons, and each drop of blood strengthened its power. The Blood Cartographers used such blades to mark the borders of Earth-side and tonight, Michael would use it once more.

He faced the wolf, drawing himself up to his full height, broadening his shoulders. He met its eyes, holding the knife out in front of him. The wolf sensed something wild within the man and backed away, slinking behind the tree. But Michael knew it would be back, along with its pack. These predators were only the forerunners of what lay beyond. They were sent as scouts, testing the boundaries of how far the Gate could be pushed open. This time, he feared it was wider than ever before.

He didn't have much time.

Michael walked to the center of the great trees, reciting the longitude and latitude of where he stood, the geographical coordinates that anchored the Gate to Earth-side. His voice grew stronger as he spoke, turning the numbers into an incantation. He planted his feet strongly upon the ground and rolled up his sleeve, baring his arm to the chill mist. The vapor curled around him, almost clawing at the scars that patterned his skin over faded tattoos. His veins ran with the pure magic of the Blood Cartographers, and now Michael knew he must call on it once again.

He put the knife against the flesh of his arm and began to carve the lines of the Gate, the circle and the crescent joined by a ley line of power as he chanted the numbers that bound this place to the physical realm. He fell to his knees, dropping the knife beside him as he dipped a finger in his wound and painted over the ground the ancient symbol of the five-pointed compass, the sigil of the Illuminated Cartographer. The storm broke overhead, the wind lashing the branches of the trees into whips that thrashed at the old man as his blood dripped upon the earth.

Michael felt his strength fading, a heaviness creeping over him as the chill mist descended. Dark powers swirled about him, and his voice faltered, hesitating as the numbers began to fade in his mind. His fingers paused over the ground, his blood dripping out. He was suddenly paralyzed, unable to speak.

A figure stepped from the trees, his features obscured by the tendrils of mist that wound around him. He wore a cloak of wolf pelt, an artifact from the Borderlands, but underneath, Michael could see he wore a suit cut from a cloth of earth. This man strode between worlds, a Shadow Cartographer, one of those who sought a new world order by remaking the maps. There was something about him, something familiar, but the mist pressed into Michael's mind, clouding his vision, making him forget.

A low growl came from behind him, and the wolf stepped from the shadows to stand by the Shadow Cartographer, its teeth bared. Behind it, the pack waited, eyes fixed on their prey.

"You're too weak this time, old man. Your kind is ending, and the Borderlanders will soon take what you have kept from them for too long."

Michael heard his words as if from afar, the sound muddled by the heavy atmosphere. In earlier times, this man would not have dared face him, but now he knew the truth. He was old and tired, his magic faded.

The wolves circled closer, sensing his weakness. Michael picked up the knife again, his movements slow as if he was underwater. The blade was heavy in his hand and strength drained from him as his blood ran onto the ground. One wolf darted in to lick at the growing pool. Michael spun with his knife, slicing at the beast but it ducked away unharmed. Another ran in to bite at his legs, its heavy body tipping him off balance. The pack formed a circle around him, teeth bared.

Two of them darted in behind, growling as they tore at his clothes, ripped through to his flesh. Michael spun again, but another two ran forward, worrying at him.

He was outnumbered.

Perhaps that had been the plan all along, after all, he was the watcher on this Gate. He thought of Bridget on her way up from the Ministry. He couldn't let her be taken as well.

He had one chance left to close the Gate, even though it would only hold a short while. But for now, it was the only way.

He looked up at the dark man watching from the shadows. He sensed triumph at the victory to come, but it would end here.

"For Galileo," Michael said, his voice strong as he spoke the words of the Illuminated Cartographer.

The wolves snarled and leapt towards their prey. Michael spun away from them, using the last of his strength to push through the pack.

He turned the blade, pressing it against his chest and hurled himself at the largest of the plane trees. Its hard trunk pushed the knife deep into his heart as Michael wrenched himself sideways, ripping himself open, falling to the ground.

Agony flashed through him as his blood pumped out, soaking the tree roots and the earth where he lay.

But the Gate was renewed by his sacrifice.

The mist curled into a vortex, and the wolves howled as they were sucked back inside the Borderlands. Michael lay panting with pain, trying to hold on long enough to watch the end.

The Shadow Cartographer stood watching him for a moment, resisting the swirl of the wind. "Your kind is ending," he whispered. "Your death only buys a little time before the change to come."

He bent to pick up Michael's five-pointed compass, then

slipped it into his pocket as he spun away, stepping back through the Gate of Shade, trailing the last of the mist behind him. The grand Georgian buildings emerged, and through the branches of the trees, Michael could see the stars above. This was his earth still, and Bath was safe.

For now.

As his blood pulsed more slowly, Michael thought of his granddaughter, Sienna. He hadn't seen her for so long, staying away in an attempt to shield her from a future he wouldn't wish on anyone. But now it seemed that she might be the only hope to close the borders for good.

CHAPTER 1

Sienna's footsteps echoed in the long corridor, acres of books in racks either side stretching into the shadows ahead of her. Dim lights came on as she walked, triggered by her movement.

It was like a bomb shelter down here. The world could be ending above ground in Oxford, but below the streets, she would be cushioned by the padding of ancient tomes. Sienna smiled, lost in thought. She could build a shelter down here in the underground stacks of the Bodleian Library. A den of ripped pages and a fire from words once considered special but now merely fuel. And she could read. Who could be lonely when there was so much to learn?

She passed into an older section of the library. The functional metal shelving changed to wooden stacks with carved lintels and wheels on the end to move them closer together. Sienna frowned. She didn't recognize this part of the library. She stopped and tugged on a cord to turn on a brighter light and bent to read the sign on the end of the nearest row. *Geopolitics of Borders and Boundaries.* She frowned and looked down at the retrieval slip in her hand. This was nowhere near where she was meant to be.

Sienna sighed. It was only her second week working in the library, and once again, she was lost. She should have turned left at Metaphysics, but she must have walked straight past the stack. By the time she retraced her steps and made it back over there, the Head Librarian would be tutting and looking at his watch, frown deepening in his furrowed brow. Books first, readers second, and lowly library clerks most definitely last. She turned and looked back the way she'd walked. The stacks stretched away, seemingly endless, darkening to shadow.

She sat down on the floor for a moment, leaning back against the shelf, sending up a cloud of dust into the air. The remains of crumbling pages, words written by those long dead, saved down here as if somehow, someone would recall them up to the rarefied air of the University once more.

She really needed to get a life.

It had been a year since leaving St Peter's College where Sienna had read Geography. Her friends had moved to jobs in London, but she hadn't been ready to leave Oxford. It had become her home over the years of study, a welcome escape from the suffocating cocoon of her mother's house. So she'd flitted around various short-term jobs and then finally landed this position, hoping it might be the right fit. But as she sat surrounded by old books, Sienna knew that this was over too.

Perhaps it was time to give in and move to London like everyone else. Perhaps she should even try again with Ben. They had been inseparable in her first two years at college, but he was a year older and got a job in the City after Finals. They'd held it together for the first year, but when she didn't move as he had expected, they began to drift apart. Right now, Sienna felt untethered, like a boat bobbing freely on the waves. She should be experiencing the exhilaration of freedom, but instead, she found herself longing for the shore. London hadn't felt like the right direction, but maybe it was time to give it another chance.

She looked at her watch and stood up again. Clutching

the retrieval slip, she retraced her steps, navigating by the signs at the end of the corridor until she found the book and hurried back to the Head Librarian's desk. He looked up as she emerged into the main vault of the Radcliffe Camera. His shaggy white eyebrows arched over his wire-rim glasses and Sienna felt his disdain rest upon her. He tapped his watch.

"Sorry," she whispered, as she placed the book on his desk. "I'm going out for my break now."

Sienna turned before he could stop her and hurried up the little stairs and out onto the steps of the Rad Cam. The air was fresh outside. Mid-June and still a little chilly, but there was a patch of sun on the other side of the square. Walking down the steps, Sienna turned on her phone, and within seconds, it started beeping with text messages and missed calls. Her mum had been calling on and off for the last hour. That was unusual. She was over-protective, but this was a lot even for her.

Sienna stood in the sun at the corner of the square by Brasenose Lane and called back.

"Hi, Mum. What's up?"

"Oh, sweetie. Something dreadful has happened. Your grandfather –" Her voice broke with a little sob.

Sienna frowned. Her mum's dad was already dead, mourned as a beloved granddad who had always shown her interesting things in the hedgerows and fields near their country house. Her father's dad was a distant memory, a man she hadn't seen or heard from since the year she started high school. He had been around after her father had disappeared, lost on a geographic survey to Antarctica, but then he'd faded into the background.

"What do you mean? What's happened?"

Her mum blew her nose. "Your grandfather's body was found this morning in Bath, just down the road from his map shop. They're saying it's some kind of ritual murder. A friend of his, Bridget, called me and told me the news. She wants to talk to you."

Shock slammed through Sienna at the words. Her grandfather murdered? It seemed impossible.

"Bridget said he left something for you, something your dad wanted you to have."

Sienna's breath caught in her throat. Ten years and the pain of losing her father still hurt, but curiosity rose at her mother's words. "Do you have her number?"

"She said you should go to Bath, to Grandad's old map shop and she would meet you there." A pause, then her mum's voice changed. "I don't think you should go, sweetie. You're working now, and you're busy. You don't want to go to that musty old map shop. It was always a complete mess when I went there with your dad back in the day. I'm sure this Bridget can send whatever it is."

Sienna half listened as she remembered being in the antique map shop as a child. The wonders of the world rendered in so many different ways. The smell of thick paper and ink, the weight and size of the maps on the wall, intricate tiny streets and imagined animals in the corners, cartouches of long-dead kings, calligraphy of names that no longer existed. Sienna remembered running her hands over the maps, feeling a vibration of energy, like they wanted her to step inside somehow. Then the concern on her dad's face, a sadness, like he wanted her to see only printed paper, not the worlds beyond the maps. After he disappeared, Mum had never taken her back there.

"I want to go," Sienna said, cutting off her mother's words.

"But what about your work?"

Sienna looked up at the dome of the Radcliffe Camera and the spires of All Souls College behind it. A gaggle of students burst from Brasenose College, chatting as they walked off to lectures.

"It's not really working out. So I'll go this afternoon. It's only a few hours on the bus to Bath."

"But I can't get down there, sweetie. You shouldn't go alone."

"I'm just going to the shop, Mum. I'm not going to visit the morgue or anything."

Her mum sighed. "Alright, but call me later. Your Grandfather was a meddler in life. I would expect him to be just as bad now he's gone."

* * *

As the bus drove through the outskirts of Bath a few hours later, Sienna gazed out the window at the fine Georgian terraces made from the distinctive honey-colored limestone that made the city famous for its architecture. Bath was smaller than Oxford, but there was a similar sense of historic weight about it. A World Heritage Site dominated by the ancient Roman Baths and a medieval Abbey, Bath had become a fashionable Georgian spa town, made famous in the books of Jane Austen.

Sienna remembered her dad talking about the background of the Farren family, how they had lived in Somerset for generations. He had only left the area because her mum had been set on London, the hub of politics surrounding their foreign aid work. But now Sienna was returning, without Dad, and with Granddad gone. The only Farren left in their line.

The bus stopped downtown, and Sienna walked up through the shops, navigating past the grand Abbey and up the hill towards The Circus. She passed a group of American tourists on the edge of Queen Square, their guide explaining loudly:

"This square marks the bottom of a key with The Circus at the top of the hill as the round end. Seen from above, it forms a Masonic shape built into the architecture of the city along with symbols of Druidic times."

His voice faded into the hubbub of the traffic as Sienna continued walking uphill towards the circle of trees visible on the rise at the end of the terrace.

As she reached the top, she paused to catch her breath, looking at the Georgian townhouses that curved around in a perfect circle. Three tiers of windows, each flanked by classical columns, rose up towards the blue sky. Stone acorn finials topped the buildings, and between each tier, a carved frieze of nautical elements, serpents and masonic symbols wove its way around. In the center of the circle, five huge plane trees stood tall on green grass, their leaves rustling in the breeze. It would have been a peaceful scene, a glimpse into a regal past, but today, bright yellow Crime Scene tape wound around the trees. Police officers stood on the perimeter, faces impassive, even as tourists took photos of the curious spectacle.

Sienna's heart thumped as she crossed the road and stood on the edge of the tape, as close as she dared go. Scene of Crime Officers still worked on the grass, but she could see between them to the trunk of the largest tree. Even from this distance, she could see it was stained with blood.

What had happened here last night? Her grandfather ran an antique map shop, so why would anyone want to hurt him? Perhaps his friend Bridget would be able to help.

Sienna turned and walked down Brock Street turning off before the Royal Crescent into Elizabeth Buildings. It was a short pedestrianized street, an eclectic mix of little shops and cafés punctuated by colorful flowers and wooden benches. She passed a curiosity shop with a maritime trunk in the window, alongside a carved wooden cross from one of the derelict churches in the nearby countryside. There was a shop selling crystals and fossils, next to a painting and craft store with glass jewelry in the window; an art gallery; a secondhand bookshop and there, in the middle, her grandfather's map shop.

While the other stores bustled with tourists, the map shop remained locked, its window in shadow. Sienna walked up and looked in at the window display. An old county map of Somerset stood in central position, its hills marked with green contoured shading. Next to it, her grandfather's book on the history of cartography, propped open by a tiny engraved globe in a wooden box. It was dark inside, but she could just make out his desk at the back, surrounded by racks of maps in plastic wrapping and the huge globe that had fascinated her as a child.

"You must be Sienna."

The voice made her jump and Sienna turned to see a woman with close-cropped dark hair standing behind. Her eyes were a piercing blue, and although the lines around them suggested the woman was over forty, she possessed an almost elfin look of mischief that made her appear younger. She wore a long dress of patchwork linen in shades of green, like the fields of the West Country in summer, interspersed with the bright yellow of rapeseed.

"I'm Bridget Ronan, a friend of your grandfather's. I recognize you from his photos. Michael had that same bright titian hair, although it looks better on you." Bridget's voice had a soft Irish lilt, and Sienna found herself immediately warming to the woman.

"Thanks for meeting me."

Bridget's welcoming smile faded. "I'm sorry for your loss, and for mine. Michael was a good friend and already sorely missed." She pulled a key from her bag. "Now, come inside." Bridget unlocked the door and pushed the door open.

Sienna walked, and as she breathed in the scent of the maps, she felt like she had come home. They called to her from the display racks, and she wanted to run her fingers over the lines, tracing the borders of the world. She walked to her grandfather's desk and turned the seventeenth-century globe a little, looking for the Barbary Coast, the area of North Africa that seemed so foreign to her when she was little. She found it and touched the picture of the apes sprawled over modern Algeria, a smile playing about her lips as she remembered the stories her grandfather told of times past.

She looked up at Bridget, who stood by the door watching her. "What happened to him?"

Bridget took a deep breath. "There's a lot we still don't know." She pulled an envelope from her bag. "But Michael gave me this to keep in case anything ever happened to him. He was nearly eighty, so he expected his time to come, although not as suddenly as this." Her eyes filled with tears as she handed Sienna the envelope. "I need to go deal with a couple of things in town, so I'll leave this with you, give you some time alone here, and I'll come back in an hour or so. Okay?"

Sienna nodded, and Bridget turned away, leaving the scent of flowers in her wake. Sienna looked down at the envelope, her name written on the front in her grandfather's spidery hand.

CHAPTER 2

THE DOORBELL TINKLED AS Bridget walked out and for a moment, Sienna just breathed in the air of the map shop. She sensed her grandfather's eye for detail in the angled lines of the wall displays, antique maps worth thousands of pounds hanging next to modern portrayals of emotional landscapes. After all, a map of the human heart is worth far more than the map of a city, she remembered him saying.

She looked down at his desk. An antique parchment map of Bath sat where he must have left it. It looked like something had spilled on the lines of The Circus, as if a red haze settled upon it. Why had he gone down there in the middle of the night?

Sienna sighed. She should have come to see him over the last years. After all, it wasn't so far to Bath, and even though her mother had kept them apart, there was no need to remain distant after going up to Oxford. He must have been lonely here, his only son dead, his only granddaughter estranged. A pang of guilt flushed through her. She should have been here for him, and now he was gone.

She opened the envelope to find one piece of cream paper inside, dated a year previously.

* * *

Dear Sienna,

As I write this, you are just finishing your degree at Oxford. I'm so proud of you, and I know your father would have been too. Geography was always his passion, as it has been mine, and I hope it can continue to be yours.

I'm sorry that we weren't able to be friends, but time and circumstance have stood between us. If you're reading this, I'm gone, and although I had hoped to spare you this, our family has always answered the call, and now it's your turn. Bridget will be able to explain more.

For now, the map shop is yours. I've arranged all the legal details, and it is in your name, along with the bank accounts and the flat above.

There will be those who try to part you from the shop, but the maps here are yours too. I hope you will remember how you felt their reality in your childhood. It's time to let that feeling emerge again, Sienna, because there is more at stake than you know.

For Galileo, and with much love,
Granddad Michael

* * *

Sienna frowned, her mind whirling with so many questions. She sat down heavily, looking up at the maps around her with new eyes. This was all hers.

She couldn't help the smile that spread across her face, even though loss resonated deep within her. It felt like coming home at last.

If she was honest, the memories of being here had driven her into studying Geography, the obsession with maps something her mother hadn't been able to remove despite emotional blackmail over the years. *Your father was lost over his obsession with maps. I won't have you go the same way.*

Her phone rang.

"Hi, Mum."

"Are you there, sweetie? Is it awful?"

"I'm here. It's fine. I met Granddad's friend, Bridget, and she gave me a letter."

A moment of silence and Sienna could sense her mother's dread. "What did it say?"

She took a deep breath. "He left me the map shop. The flat, the bank accounts. Even though I hadn't seen him for years. It's so strange."

"Well, that's wonderful news because you can sell it and use the money to pay off your loans and get a new start in London." Sienna tuned out as her mother rattled on about how much she could get for a place in central Bath and how lucky she was, and it was good because her father didn't leave anything and on and on.

Sienna looked around at the maps and felt them calling to her again. She stood and went to one of the racks, leafing through them as she made agreeable noises. On some of the maps, her fingers trembled against a kind of magnetic field from the paper even through the plastic sleeves that covered them. It was strange, and yet, it also felt natural. Some of the maps didn't have this effect. Maybe there was something in the paper? Perhaps Bridget would be able to help, as her grandfather had suggested.

"So, do you want me to contact the estate agents?" Her mother's voice broke through. "There's one just around the corner from you. I could get it sorted tomorrow."

"No, I need to wait a little, Mum. Let me sort this out myself."

"Well, don't wait too long. That street must look beautiful with the summer flowers out. It's a very good time to sell."

The doorbell tinkled again. Sienna turned to see a tall man enter, his frame erect, his back straight in an almost military fashion. He was distinguished, salt and pepper hair swept back from an angular face, with a patrician nose and thin lips. A vertical scar ran down from his right eye to his short beard, the skin pale and puckered around the old wound. He wore a tailored three-piece suit in English tweed and looked as if he'd just stepped out of one of the paintings from the Holburne Museum.

"I've got to go, Mum. I'll call you later." Sienna hung up and turned to the man. "Morning, can I help you?"

The man looked at her, eyes narrowing for a moment, then he smiled in recognition. "I was looking for Michael." His accent was impeccable Queen's English. "But you must be his granddaughter. I've seen pictures of you. Sienna, is it?" He reached out a hand. "I'm Sir Douglas Mercator."

Sienna stepped forward and shook his hand, meeting his grey eyes, the color of a wolf pelt. His grip was firm, his hand cool and although he was charming, there was something about him that made her take a step back. She felt rather than heard a rustle in the maps around her. "My grandfather isn't here. He … He died yesterday."

Saying the words aloud made Sienna flinch as if it made real something that had only been an idea before.

Sir Douglas' gaze didn't drop; his expression didn't falter. "Oh, I'm so sorry for your loss. You must have a lot to sort out here." He stepped forward and ran his hand over one of the maps displayed on the countertop. It was covered in glass, but Sienna thought she could smell burning, as if his touch singed the edges.

He turned back, pulled a business card from his jacket pocket and handed it to her. "I'm a dealer in antique maps, like your grandfather was." The card was embossed in gold, the word Mercator entwined with a projection of the globe.

"Oh, of course." Sienna shook her head in apology.

"Sorry, I didn't recognize your name at first. Are you related to the Flemish cartographer?"

Sir Douglas nodded. "Yes, I'm a direct descendant. Our family have been in the map trade since his day." He looked around the shop, his eyes alight with interest. "I knew your father as well. He was my contemporary when we studied Geography at Oxford. I believe it is your alma mater, too?"

Sienna nodded, a little in awe of the man. After all, he was cartographic royalty.

"With Michael gone, and your father too, perhaps the shop is yours now?" His voice changed, and Sienna sensed a covetousness behind his charm. "I've been trying to buy this shop from Michael for years. He was too old to run it well of late, and I have clients who would be interested in some of the maps. I can offer you a very good deal, Sienna. You'd have more money than you need and I'd handle everything for you. This is my world, after all." He smiled, but it didn't reach his eyes. "I'm sure you have a lot to think about, so keep my card and call me if you'd like to sell. Or even to offload some of this stock." He waved a hand around at the maps.

"Thank you. I'll definitely think about it."

Sir Douglas gave her a long look, then nodded and swept out of the shop. Sienna sensed the space exhale as if it had been holding itself in check while he was present. She went over to the map he had touched, and sure enough, around the edges, faint charring had appeared, dark patches of soot as if it had been burned. She shook her head. What was going on here?

Sienna went to the door and locked it, turning the sign to Closed. She didn't need any more unexpected visitors, and she wanted to look at the flat upstairs. Behind the desk at the back of the shop, a narrow wooden staircase wound up to the first floor. The stairs creaked as she walked up, the language of an old building, and she thought about her grandfather walking up here, footsteps heavy after a day's work.

At the top, a faded red wooden door etched with a curious five-pointed compass blocked the way. Sienna tried several of the keys until one fitted the lock and she walked in.

She had expected a musty old place, somewhere you'd expect an eighty-year-old to live, but her breath caught as she emerged into a wide open-plan living space. The walls had been opened up into archways, with picture windows looking out over the street on one side and a little courtyard at the back. A stylish kitchen and tasteful furniture made it into a modern flat, the type of place she'd only seen in magazines. Nothing like the chaos of her mother's house, packed to the gunnels with chests and boxes and bags. This was a haven and Sienna exhaled, relaxing into it.

One long wall of shelves was piled high with books, and she stepped closer to see what they were. *The Atlas of Improbable Places*, books of photos from abandoned cities, and a shelf of journals. They were all black, leather-bound hardbacks in the same A5 size, each with an elastic band to hold loose papers inside. They were dated on the spine, one per year going back to the 1950s.

Sienna's heart pounded as she considered them. They were her grandfather's private words, but he was gone, and after all, he'd left them here out in the open. She pulled one from the shelf and leafed through the pages. His handwriting was almost illegible, but it wasn't the words that caught her eye, it was the hand-drawn maps and sketches inside. The pencil lines were exact and confident, line drawings of temples next to a rough street map. She recognized the name of the place, but it didn't make sense. Babylon, a ruined city lost in time, but here, her grandfather had drawn it as if it were still alive, as if he had explored its streets.

The journals only added more questions to the many she already had. Sienna sat back and looked around her at the light and airy flat. It already felt like home. The job wasn't working out in Oxford anyway, so perhaps she should move here. Let Sir Douglas sell the shop and keep this part, or rent it, or something. There were suddenly so many options. She needed a coffee.

There was a little café over the street, so Sienna headed back downstairs, out the door and over to the Green Door. It bustled with customers, and the familiar smell of ground coffee filled the air. A young woman with pink curly hair and glitter in her eyebrows smiled in greeting as she arranged sweet pastries on the countertop.

"What can I get you, my lovely?" Her broad West Country accent made Sienna smile. Bath was in Somerset, after all, home of cider, rolling hills and Cheddar cheese.

"Just a black Americano, thanks."

As the young woman made the coffee, Sienna looked around at the place. Students worked on laptops as two men engaged in a heated business discussion in one corner, while a well-preserved older lady read the paper opposite them. Sienna wondered if her grandfather had sat here sometimes, and a pang of regret shot through her at opportunities lost.

She took her coffee out to the street and walked down Elizabeth Buildings towards Brock Street, wanting to catch the last rays of the sun. At the end, she turned towards the Royal Crescent where a group of tourists stood on the edge of the green lawn of Royal Victoria Park. Families sat enjoying the sun, playing games and laughing.

Sienna looked both ways and glimpsed a young, mixed-race woman walking a golden cocker spaniel on the opposite side of the road. The little dog looked up and started wagging its tail as it saw her just as a double-decker tourist bus turned the corner. It sped towards them, going too fast for the little streets. The spaniel ran out suddenly into the road, barking in excitement, its eyes fixed upon Sienna.

"Zippy! Come back!" the young woman shouted as the bus barreled down on them.

CHAPTER 3

SIENNA DROPPED HER COFFEE and stepped into the road.

She swept the little dog up into her arms as the bus horn blared and she darted back to the pavement. The spaniel licked her face, and she laughed, heart pounding at the near miss, wondering what the hell had made her step in front of a bus for a random dog.

The young woman crossed over the road. She was early twenties, similar to Sienna's age, but her features were a dark opposite. Her black curls were cropped close, her eyes almond-shaped with high arched eyebrows. She wore a plain black t-shirt and jeans, and she had tattoos down one arm. A globe intertwined with geographical symbols and a five-pointed compass, just like the one on her grandfather's door.

"I'm so sorry," the woman said. "He suddenly pulled out of my grip when he saw you." Sienna cuddled the little dog close as he nuzzled her neck. The woman frowned. "It's odd though, he doesn't do that with many people. Do we know you?"

Sienna shook her head. "I've just arrived." She pointed back down the street. "The map shop was my grandfather's."

The young woman's eyes widened in recognition. "You're Michael's granddaughter?"

"You knew him?"

She nodded. "Of course, yes. Oh, my goodness. I'm so sorry about his death." Sienna thought she could see more than just regret in the woman's eyes. Did she know something more? "Did you see Bridget already?"

"Yes, she gave me a key for the shop. Does everyone know everyone here?"

The young woman laughed. "It's a small city, and the map community is tight knit, for sure." She put out a hand. "I'm Mila Wendell."

Sienna put Zippy down and shook Mila's hand. "Sienna Farren."

"I helped your granddad out in the shop sometimes and often manned his stall at the map fairs in London if he was too tired to travel."

Her words cut through Sienna. She should have been the one helping. "I met Sir Douglas Mercator as well. You must know him?"

Mila's expression darkened. "Yes, of course. He's ... Well, he doesn't usually come around this part of town much. He and your grandfather didn't get on. Actually, that's an understatement. What did he want?"

Sienna turned back towards Elizabeth Buildings. "To buy the shop."

Mila shook her head. "The old bastard's been trying to take it over for years. But before you make a decision, you should know a bit more about what Michael stood for. Did you find his compass?"

Sienna shook her head. "No, Bridget just gave me a letter."

"I know where it's kept. I can show you if you like. I know he'd want you to have it."

Together, they walked back to the map shop. Mila tied Zippy to a bench outside, and he lay down facing the shop, clearly used to the place. When they walked in, Sienna felt the maps warm to them both, and she sensed that Mila was welcome here. She didn't know how she knew it, and there were more questions piling up, but for now, Sienna was just glad to have someone around who knew her grandfather and seemed to love the shop.

Mila walked over to a chest of drawers with a glass display cabinet on top. "Michael kept some of the most precious maps here, away from sticky wandering fingers." She looked up. "Do you know anything about maps, about how much this is all worth?"

Sienna shook her head. "I studied Geography but it wasn't so much about maps, and I don't know anything about the antique or collectable side." She paused, looking around at what was left of her father's side of the family. "But I want to learn."

Mila met her eyes and then she nodded. "There's more to learn than you think." She knelt down and pulled a round wooden box out of the drawer, frowning as she felt its weight. She pulled the lid off to reveal an empty velvet case. Mila's face fell. "They must have taken it from him."

"Who? The people who killed Granddad?" Sienna knelt down next to her. "Do you know who it was?"

Mila took a deep breath. "It's complicated. I don't know what to tell you about his death, but a Cartographer's compass is his most treasured possession."

Sienna stood up. "This is all so crazy. This morning I woke up in Oxford and everything was fine, and now I'm here, and Granddad is gone. Murdered. I have this shop, but I also have an offer for it. Should I just take the money and run?"

Mila smiled softly. "If your life is elsewhere, then of course. I know Michael would understand. He would have wanted you to have a full life without the weight of family expectation. Bridget can help you sell the place if it's what you want."

Mila's words struck a chord because she didn't have a life

elsewhere. Not really. Sienna knew she'd been aimless and wandering for too long, unable to choose a path forward. Her father had made his choices and paid the ultimate price. Her grandfather too had met his end because of something to do with the maps. Her curiosity burned to know more, but there was a touch of fear there too. If she walked away now, she could go to London, patch things up with Ben, start anew with money in her pocket, student loans paid off, maybe even have enough to buy a place. And yet …

She touched the maps in the case before her, sensing a texture in the air around them, like running her hand through a field of wheat. There was something anchoring her here, and she wanted to know what the hell was going on, why Granddad died, and how there could possibly be sketches of long-dead cities in his journals upstairs.

Mila walked over to the globe and spun it around a little way. "Michael kept your ancestral history from you, but perhaps it's time for you to make your own map, Sienna."

The doorbell rang again. Bridget walked in and smiled to see Mila. "I'm glad you two found each other already."

"Zippy saw to that." Mila laughed, then she turned serious, indicating the empty case. "Michael's compass is gone."

Bridget frowned. "Then things are going to get worse. Sienna, I know you're confused. Michael tried to keep you away from all this, but now you have to know. Come with me to the Ministry of Maps. Come and see what your grandfather worked on. And your father too."

"My father? You knew him?"

Bridget nodded and her eyes softened in remembrance. "John and I trained together. We were … friends before he was lost. There are many things for you to know if you want to."

Sienna's phone buzzed. She pulled it out and looked at the name on the screen. It was her mother again. She wouldn't want her daughter getting involved. But something tugged at Sienna. She had to know.

She rejected the call. "I'll come with you. But I haven't made up my mind about keeping the shop yet."

Bridget nodded. "Of course."

Sienna grabbed her bag, and they left the shop. Zippy jumped around, nuzzling against Sienna's leg as Mila untied him. "He likes you. He adored Michael, too, but right now, I need to take him back to the boat. I'll meet you at the Ministry later." She headed off up the hill.

"So what is this Ministry?" Sienna asked.

"Suspend your rational side for a moment," Bridget said as they walked. "It can be hard to fathom, but we have to start somewhere." She took a deep breath. "Bath has two different sides. The city is a World Heritage Site with two thousand-year-old Roman Baths, the medieval Abbey, Georgian architecture and boutique shopping. That's what most people see. But it also has an unseen dimension you won't find on any terrestrial maps. It's a portal to the Borderlands, a place where this earth bleeds into another. There are other portals in ancient places where borders blur: Athens, Rome, Damascus, Varanasi, Jerusalem. Places where people have been written in and out of history. The Ministry protects the borders, and it keeps the Borderlands from slipping back over here."

They emerged into The Circus side by side, the police still working in the center. Bridget sighed. "Your grandfather worked for the Ministry, and this is where the border opened last night. He stopped whatever might have come through. He gave his life to protect the city, not that most people can ever know about it."

Sienna heard her words and saw the bloody tree, but how could this be real? Her mind reeled with questions. They walked around the edge and headed down the hill past the shops and the Bertinet bakery, past the Guildhall, until they reached the Abbey Church of Saint Peter and Saint Paul, known locally as Bath Abbey. Its Gothic presence dominated the central city, a hub for tourists and photographers for its carved facade of climbing angels and ornate wooden door. The Bath stone glowed with a golden light as the late sun touched the tower. Bridget paused as they reached the thick walls and they stood for a moment under the flying buttresses and magnificent stained glass windows.

"The Abbey was built on a pagan site, founded as a convent, then turned into a monastery in the seventh century. It's been rebuilt several times, grander with every incarnation. The Ministry is based in the levels beneath and in some of the surrounding buildings. We also have a training facility up at the University on the hill."

"Why here?" Sienna asked.

"Bath is an ancient energy center," Bridget explained. "With the confluence of ley lines that run across Britain, the river and the underground hot springs, it has drawn people through the ages. The Freemasons in the Georgian period concentrated the energy into The Circus and so the Ministry is here to protect the area."

"Is it part of the church?"

Bridget shook her head. "Not in a religious fashion, but our facility is wound into the structure of the Abbey. You'll see when we go below."

She lead Sienna round the back of the Abbey, past the inscription marking where the first king of all England, Edgar, was crowned in 973 AD. A statue of the risen Christ emerging from the grave, shroud bandages still around him, stood marking an entranceway with thick stone steps down to a tiny door.

"It doesn't look like much," Bridget said. "But wait until you get inside."

Sienna followed her down. At first, it seemed the stone steps must lead into some equally ancient crypt, but Bridget turned when they reached the bottom and faced the stone wall.

"You can walk on into the museum below the church, but the Ministry is this way."

She touched a groove in the wall, and the stone cracked open. The outline of a door emerged, and Bridget pushed against it. On the other side, there was a library, the walls lined with books of maps and easy chairs placed next to low tables for reading. Sienna didn't recognize many of the names on the spines and part of her longed to stay here and escape into the tomes. But Bridget marched straight through, entering a code on a door on the other side and leading her on.

They emerged into a long hallway with doors leading off it, each labeled with a different title. Antiquities, Restoration, Misinformation, Illustration. They passed one door stained a deep red with the words *Blood Gallery* etched into the wood.

Sienna took a step towards it, but Bridget held her arm. "That's not for you just yet. There will be time to learn it all if you choose, but first, you must meet the Illuminated Cartographer. This way."

The corridor walls were full of photographs, exuberant faces of explorers around the world. As they walked by, Sienna scanned them for a glimpse of her family. She stopped in front of one where her grandfather stood in front of the temple he had sketched in his journal. "Is it really Babylon?" she asked.

Bridget turned and came back to look. "Yes, I know it's hard to understand. But there are places that have been lost Earth-side, but remain in the Borderlands. Some of us cross those borders through special maps. We are Mapwalkers, Sienna. Mila and me. Your grandfather. Your father."

Sienna turned at her words. "Is there a picture of him?"

Bridget nodded and walked along a little, searching amongst the faces. "Here."

Sienna looked up at the picture. Her dad stood with four

others, two men and two women. His face was broad with a smile, his titian hair shining in the sun, his beard longer than she'd ever seen it. He wore khaki shorts and held a bulging backpack. Behind the group, what looked like a South American city stretched into green jungle. Sienna touched his face with a fingertip.

"I don't even have a grave to visit."

Bridget looked surprised. "Of course not. Your father isn't dead."

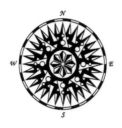

CHAPTER 4

MILA WALKED ALONG THE canal path, Zippy running along next to her, excited to be out in the warmth of the afternoon. He sniffed in the hedgerows and snuffled in the reeds as a pair of iridescent dragonflies flitted about his head. Mila thought about Sienna. The young woman didn't know anything about her Mapwalker heritage and it made Mila wonder what her own life would have been like if she'd never known.

A robin trilled in the hedgerows by her side, then the peep-peep of new ducklings came from the canal as the little balls of fluff paddled fast beside her hoping for a crumb. With every step, she was grateful. Grateful that she wasn't in London, in the tower block she grew up in, where she could barely walk a meter or so along the corridor. She used to run up and down the flights of stairs just to expend some of her energy, and to stay away from the other kids in her foster family. Although the word family barely applied, at least it was a roof over her head. She didn't know much about her birth parents, only hints that her father had been a student from war-torn Sierra Leone. In London, mixed-race was normal, but here in Bath, her darker skin and almond-shaped eyes stood out and sometimes, she liked being different.

Back then, Mila would escape to the canals of London, walking for hours alongside the slow-moving water. She longed to get in, to let the cool slide over her body. She wanted to open her mouth and let it flood into her lungs, to slit open her wrists and let her blood mingle with the canal, become one with it.

Sometimes she would go down to the Thames, past the great buildings of the old city, where the river swept towards the sea. It was wild and untamed and although she was drawn to it, Mila knew that if she were to dive into the water, she would lose herself. There were creatures in the ocean, beasts that would hurt her, whereas in the canal, there were only tiny fish, lithe water voles and diving ducks. A tamer form of escape.

After she left school, she traveled along the canal system, getting odd jobs now and then, helping out and learning the ropes from the other travelers, finding a new form of family among the canal boat people. She had saved up for her own boat and one day, found herself here in Bath, where she met Bridget who recognized her Mapwalker ability.

And now, every day she would walk here, along the Kennet and Avon Canal, away from Bath towards Bradford-on-Avon, a nature walk within hailing distance of the city. Seasons changed but the rhythm of the canal pulsed through her life. She knew this earth, this water and something was definitely wrong. Michael's murder had disturbed the equilibrium of the city, and Mila felt the tendrils of dark mist reach even here. She sighed and Zippy ran back to her, his dark eyes looking up with devotion.

"Good boy." She reached down to rub the soft fur around his ears. "Stay close now."

They walked on under a bridge built from thick blocks of stone, her footsteps echoing as she walked through. The coo of a wood pigeon boomed out as the sun dappled through the leaves of the horse chestnut trees at the waterside. A cloud of midges hung over the reeds next to a patch of purple clover and white flowers of wild garlic. The smell was a heady scent of summer as she walked along the bank next to sycamore trees and hedgerows of dog roses where blackberries would grow later in the autumn. Mila scanned the area, letting her senses spread out over the waterway, trying to pinpoint the source of her disturbance.

Water rippled as fish rose to feed on the midges. In the field above the canal, two great shire horses with shaggy feet stood grazing. A bell tinkled behind her and Mila moved to one side as a cyclist zoomed past. Zippy barked in greeting and ran alongside it a little way until returning to walk at her side. Mila smiled down at him. He gave her a reason to be on land, not mapwalking through the waterways all the time.

A friend on a boat further down the canal looked after him when she was away. A woodturner who roved the canal paths after storms, looking for branches to carve into animal shapes and bowls. Zippy was apparently a great helper in retrieving wood but Mila was always happiest when he was back with her. She loved being with Zippy, his quiet devotion, his lack of judgement for who she was or what she did. She missed him when she went into the Borderlands, but if he crossed over, he wouldn't make it back. He would be lost over there, as sometimes she felt she might be.

When Mila mapwalked the waterways, she became one with the canal and lost a part of herself. Sometimes she thought she would never emerge, that she could stay in there forever. Perhaps the water nymphs of old were born this way? Myths of women who lived in water and came out to tempt the sailors. She had read about them in a library book once. Perhaps her father had really been Neptune, great god of the sea. Mila smiled to herself to think she could actually be an ocean princess, rather than a poor foster child from a London tower block.

It was this search for identity that always drove her back

to the Ministry, even though she didn't really fit in there. The other trainees were from special families, those who understood their Mapwalking lineage. She was seen as some kind of throwback, a line that had branched off early. Mila wondered if perhaps back in Sierra Leone, she might find people like her. But she'd never been. She'd never left England, never gone to seek her father's heritage or find others like her, Africans who traveled by water. Perhaps that's what drew her to Sienna, who seemed to know even less about her own ability.

They walked on past a ginger cat lying in a patch of sun on a boat piled high with the detritus of living, a rusty wheelbarrow, logs of wood for the winter. It looked up sleepily as they passed, nonplussed by Zippy's exuberance. Mila nodded her head, acknowledging him as part of this world. In the Borderlands last time, she'd seen a cat there, but it had been misshapen, its eyes rheumy, weeping, diseased.

Mila walked on, past the graveyard next to the road, full of stone markers, Celtic crosses, and headstones marking the passing of time. The Bathampton Church was solid, squatting on the land like it would always be there. But Mila had seen others like it in the Borderlands, those where congregations had died and left the building derelict until the border had claimed it, rewriting it out of this history and into the alternate.

The rules were to always go into the Borderlands as a team. That was the official word, but Mila went over alone sometimes when she felt the need to be on the edge. The Mapwalkers went into the Borderlands to retrieve artifacts lost or deliberately written out but now needed back on Earth-side. The things they brought back were kept in the Ministry vaults. But when Mila sometimes traveled alone into those places, she brought back tiny things, shells or stones, coins sometimes, and she kept them on her boat, evidence of another place where perhaps she felt more at home.

Bridget had said she shouldn't keep things, shouldn't mark herself as a Mapwalker, that there were people who could track her because of those objects, that she left a part of herself behind if she went over too much. Maybe she was turning feral, turning Borderlander.

Mila passed a pair of swans with five cygnets nibbling at the grass at the side of the canal. The smell of elderflower lingered in the air, as the chirps of birds came from the hedgerows. She had walked in wild places in the Borderlands similar to this, but the foliage was different. It was as if the land there had crossed from the edges of the map in different cultures, growing strange plants, turning animals into different versions of themselves.

A thrush flew from the hedgerow, a snail in its beak, darting under the weeping willow on the opposite bank. The cluck-cluck of chickens came from one of the smallholdings just off the path. Mila passed a canal boat with a kneeling river goddess on top, her arms outstretched to welcome the day, a laughing Buddha by her side. A tangle of spiderwebs on the guide ropes glistened in the sun.

It seemed idyllic but something was definitely wrong.

Mila bent and put her hand down into the canal water, closing her eyes as she sensed the movement of the ripples and the deeper current as it swept towards the city and on to the river. Over time she had become attuned to the difference of the Borderlands, how her skin felt as she moved from bright sunlight to shade. And she sensed it now.

The border was being tested.

She stood up. "Zippy, come."

The spaniel darted to her side, bouncing up and down as they turned and walked quickly back towards town, back to where the canal ran alongside the manicured gardens of the Holburne Museum.

They kept walking until the canal emerged alongside allotments, little gardens where city dwellers grew vegetables and flowers. Their personalities were evident in the plots, some with colored buckets and different types of flowers, rows of runner beans on poles next to hollyhocks and poppies. One area had a blue gate with five bars, just a gate on two poles with no fence. It was unusual, but always made Mila smile as she passed. The pride people had in these little gardens in the heart of the city made her even more fiercely determined to protect it.

She walked on towards the lock, where the canal changed level. Water could be let in and out with heavy gates and the boat would move up or down as the canal rose and fell with the gradient of the land. The locks had scared her at first and she had avoided moving her own boat for fear of getting trapped in one, but now they were part of her life here. Mila heard a noise further on, a bubbling and boiling sound that filled her heart with dread.

The border was being breached.

A wild squawking of ducks came from up ahead and she raced towards the noise, Zippy by her side. They rounded a corner just past the end of the lock gate.

At the edge of the canal, the water bubbled ferociously. There was a smell in the air, the scent of a bombed-out city, spent ammunition and decay overpowering the earthy scent of nature. How could they breach here now? The thought flashed through Mila's mind as a man burst up out of the water. She could see by the half-moon tattoo on his face that he was one of the warlord's men, a Feral Borderlander. The man began to swim to shore.

CHAPTER 5

Bridget's words rocked through Sienna. Her heart pounded, her mind whirling. "What do you mean, he's not dead? My mum said he was lost on a mission to Antarctica."

Bridget sighed. "Your mother never knew what John really did. He kept his Mapwalking secret. He wanted to protect you both."

Sienna shook her head. "I can't believe it." That her father might still be alive was one thing, but that he purposefully let her believe him dead seemed unthinkable. She had so many questions but at least there was some hope she might see him again.

Bridget put a hand out and touched Sienna's arm. "It's true. I don't know what else to say. John was lost a month ago on the edge of the Uncharted, along with the rest of the Extreme Cartographic Force. It's a place of wild magic, beyond the Borderlands where the Shadow Cartographers rule." Bridget shook her head. "They should never have gone so far out, but there were rumors about a Map of Shadows being created there." She turned away. "They never came back. Time warps the further out you go in the Uncharted, so he could have been lost only yesterday in his time."

"So there's nothing I can do in order to find him?"

Bridget smiled. "We'll see." She turned away down the

hall. "You will know your path when the way forks before you."

Her words resounded in Sienna, an echo of something her father had said long ago. Words he had written on her heart. He had clearly wanted her to stay away from this place, but now she needed to know more. If he was still alive, she might somehow see him again. She hurried after Bridget.

They walked down a long corridor hung with tapestries. The maps were recognizable as European, but the contours were wrong, the lines off in some places. Bridget saw her looking. "These are maps of what was and perhaps what will be again."

"What do you mean?"

"People trust that the maps they see in books and pictures are true. They rarely question whether they match the real world. But what is more real? The map in your geography textbook or the world you walk upon with your own feet."

"But you can't know the shape of a land by walking it. You're too close to the ground," Sienna noted.

Bridget smiled. "Exactly, and the borders of these lands have been remade by those who draw the maps. The Cartographers. We make the borders and we have to keep redrawing the maps. There is no status quo. The Borderlanders are always shifting as new places are pushed through."

She pointed to the tapestries. "Maps are not an exact representation of the world, merely a worldview of the creator. For example, there are some maps that don't have Israel on them, others that have no Palestine. All you have to do is erase a name or change a line if you wish to wipe a nation off the map, or create a new one. Look at how the Sykes-Picot line changed the Middle East. Sykes drew his finger across a map, drawing a line that continues to shape modern day. Yet those lines didn't represent people's tribal allegiances, just an ideology."

Suddenly, a whooshing sound echoed down the corridor, like the explosive belch of air as a fire bursts from a furnace.

"Oh no, not again." Bridget ran towards the sound, Sienna following close behind. They reached a thick metal door, riveted with huge bolts and a reinforced glass window in the side. They peered inside.

A young man stood in the blackened room with his back turned, his clothes charred. His shoulders were slumped, and Sienna sensed his disappointment. He wore a blue t-shirt and jeans, but they were patchy with burned holes. He was tall and slender, his arms lightly muscled and now covered in ash. Before him on the table was a map that looked completely unharmed by the flames, if indeed there had been any, because there were none there now.

"Perry is struggling to harness his fire magic," Bridget explained as she knocked on the window.

The young man turned, his ice-blue eyes widening as he saw them. His face looked as if it had been carved from porcelain, so perfect were his features, his lips full with a patrician nose. His short blonde hair was singed and sooty. He made the okay signal with his finger and thumb and gave Sienna a wink as Bridget turned away.

"Luckily, the room is made for fire practice."

"What exactly is he doing?" Sienna asked as they continued to walk.

"There are different types of magic. The fire element enables the Mapwalker to destroy maps in order to remake them, so it's a blend of destruction and creation. Fire can rejuvenate, some seed pods open only in the heat of a flame, some species live only because others die. Those like Perry can walk in smoke and flame and travel in the seams of energy in the earth." Bridget sighed. "There's a strong fire faction in the Shadow Cartographers, so we're lucky to have Peregrine. Of course, as long as he can master it before the next mission."

"Mission?"

"We're training a new Extreme Cartographic Force. The Map of Shadows is a way to remake the borders, to write us out of history. The mission is to retrieve it from the Borderlands."

"So this team are going after my father?"

Bridget frowned. "Following his footsteps, for sure, but this time, we don't intend to lose anyone in the process."

They arrived at another door carved from a light ash inscribed with a globe. Bridget turned to Sienna. "What you see in here is as true as the maps in your grandfather's shop. Remember that."

Her words puzzled Sienna, and she frowned as Bridget pushed open the door and they stepped into the room.

For so deep under the ground, the room was incredibly bright, filled with mirrors reflecting light into even the farthest corners. It was a library of sorts, but instead of books, the shelves were full of rolled maps, some tiny and frayed, others the size of a rolled carpet. They spilt onto the floor in piles, like a hoarder's den. It smelled of cedar wood, tea and a hint of spices, of rose water and Turkish delight, like a Middle Eastern souk with an endless array of delight for the senses. There was a path through the maze of maps, and a rustling sound came from deeper inside the room.

"Is that you, Bridget?"

A man emerged from the pile as if he had been sleeping amongst the maps. His craggy face was etched with lines as deep as the caves under the Mendip hills, and as he moved, the maps moved with him. He was connected to them, they wound into him and through him, his blood inking the pages.

"They call me the Illuminated Cartographer," he said, and his voice crackled like the maps around him. "I am bound to this room, the beating heart of the maps. But once I walked as free as Bridget here." His dark eyes crinkled as he smiled. "I knew your father, Sienna, and I hope I will get to know you. After all, your place has always been here." He frowned. "Now there is something I have to give you." He spun around, the maps winding themselves around him. The colors changed as if the symbols morphed with his mood. "But I don't know quite where it is."

He walked away from them, pausing at a huge shelf with rows of rolled maps. A ladder leaned against it. "I'm getting too old for this." He looked back at Sienna. "Why don't you go up and get it, my dear?"

Sienna looked up at the miles of shelves. She thought she could spend forever in here, delving into interesting corners, but there was clearly something the Illuminated Cartographer wanted her to see.

She walked through the rustle of maps to the ladder and climbed up. Symbols marked each shelf she passed, the runes of the Mapwalkers. Some she recognized and others were foreign, evoking images of words whispered in forgotten places.

"A bit higher and to your right."

Sienna reached a shelf near the ceiling marked with a row of stars.

"Yours is there, child." There was a hint of regret in his voice as if he didn't want her to see whatever it was. And yet, she was here.

She leaned out to her right, looking down to the ground below. She had a fleeting thought that she could jump and land cushioned on the maps below, like a huge bouncy castle. Or she might just crack her head open on the floor. She turned back to the shelf.

The rolled maps had names written on them in tiny writing. Peregrine Mercator. Was he the guy in the fire room and was he related to Sir Douglas, the man who wanted her father's shop? Xander Temple. Mila Wendell. And then her name. Sienna Farren. What the hell?

"The children of the Mapwalkers," the Illuminated Cartographer called up to her. "We map your star charts at birth and store them here. These charts go back generations, Sienna. You are here, as well as your father, your grandfather and those who came before."

"Why?"

"If you are lost, it is your last way home, back to the place where your stars aligned."

Sienna pulled her map from the shelf, wrapping one arm around the ladder to hold herself in place as she unrolled it. A star chart was tattooed on the smooth vellum, dots of stars anchoring her to a specific time and place. In the corner was a five-pointed compass rose, the decoration matching her father's compass that she remembered playing with as a child. Sienna looked down the rows of rolled vellum stretching into the distance. Who were all these other Mapwalkers and how far back did this lineage go?

Suddenly an alarm rang out, the lights around her flashing red, casting the room in a bloody glow.

* * *

Mila knew that where there was one Feral, more would follow. When these wild Borderlanders crossed over, they usually sent a scout first. If the scout didn't come back, well, there were plenty more where he came from. This one was young, only a teenager, younger than she was.

She stood back in the shadow of the lock gate, waiting, watching. As far as she knew, the warlord's men had never come through this far away from The Circus and that in itself was worrying. If they were finding new places, new rips in the border, then they could come through anywhere. Perhaps even further out in the countryside where no one was watching. Ministry protocol dictated that she should call this in right now and wait for backup, but the canal was her home, and she would not allow the Borderlanders through here.

The man swam towards the bank.

Mila knelt down and put her hand in the canal water at the side of the lock, feeling the cool flow touch her skin. It rippled through her body as her connection with the water expanded.

The man had almost reached the side. She had to stop him.

As his fingers touched the bank, Mila slipped into the water without so much as a ripple in her wake. She became one with the liquid, sliding sinuously through the darkness of the canal, her senses attuned to the invader. Slipping past him, Mila grabbed his leg, tugging him away from the lip of the canal before he could get out. His muffled cry came from above as she pulled him underwater, slipped on past, turned with an undulation and then came back for him.

In these moments, Mila felt like any hunter. The thrill of the chase, the knowledge of strength. The pity she might have felt for the Feral subsided under a need to protect what was hers. And this canal was hers, no doubt about it.

The man flailed in the water, trying to paddle to the shore again, his breath ragged. Mila slid past again and pulled him down under the water. He wrestled with her, his fingers sliding over her skin smooth as silk, part of the water.

She propelled herself down, dragging him towards a patch of weed that grew at the edge of the canal, taking him down. He kicked and flailed harder now, desperate for air. Silt rose around them in a cloud as Mila thrust him to the bottom. She took a handful of weed and wound it around his neck, anchoring him to the canal floor. His mouth pursed, desperate not to breathe and then he couldn't help himself. As she tightened the weed around his neck, he opened his mouth. The water poured in. He kicked and fought, eyes bulging.

Mila wondered if there was someone waiting for him back in the Borderlands. What would they do when he didn't return? She hovered in the water above him, watched his eyes go blank, his body go limp.

He wasn't her first, and he wouldn't be her last. Mila would do this again and again to stop them coming through. She thought of the allotments above, the flowers and the hedgerows of the canal as she tightened the weed around the man's neck to keep his body down. The Ministry team would come and sort out the remains later. Ferals from the Borderland had no identity on this side, so it wasn't murder. It was defense.

This was war.

Mila slipped away and pulled herself out of the canal. She shook the water off like an animal as Zippy ran to her side, jumping up and barking in excitement. "It's okay, boy. We're alright."

She sat down on the bank to catch her breath, Zippy nuzzling into her lap. Mila watched the water go by as a heron fished in the quiet shade of a willow tree.

CHAPTER 6

THE NOISE OF THE alarm echoed around the Illuminated Cartographer's library.

"Come down quickly," Bridget called up. "I need to get to the War Room."

Sienna hurried back down the ladder, clutching the star map to her chest. At the bottom, the Illuminated Cartographer held out a hand. "You can't take it with you now. It belongs here until such time as you go into the Borderlands."

"But I –"

"We need to go now." Bridget stood by the door, one hand holding it open as she beckoned.

Sienna hurried after her but turned at the door, looking back at the old man tethered to the map room, his life blood sustaining the core of the Ministry. He smiled at her, and in his eyes, she saw a promise of something she didn't quite grasp yet. Had those same eyes smiled at her father as he left?

"Let's go," Bridget said. "The alarm means there's been another breach. Stay close now."

Bridget hurried through the corridors, twisting left and right until Sienna was unsure how far they'd come or if they'd just doubled back on themselves multiple times.

They reached an open door leading into a wide room with a huge table in the middle. Above it spun a three-dimensional computer model of Bath, The Circus in the middle. It pulsed with a dim light as if some power hummed beneath. Mist hovered at its center while moving dots ranged out from the darkness. Another light flashed scarlet by the canal.

A group of people stood around the table, all talking at once, pointing at charts on the walls around them. The hum of voices coalesced into one, but Sienna heard snatches of the conversation.

"Multiple breaches …"

"Feral wolves …"

"Fatality on the canal …"

Bridget called for silence, and Sienna stood back a little, watching as the Irish woman took control of the situation. She turned to a man holding a tablet. It looked to be running some kind of mapping software. "Status update, please, Jerod."

The man adjusted his glasses. "There are multiple breaches this time. Mist descended on The Circus about twenty minutes ago, and the howling of feral wolves has been heard. Police investigators were already on the scene because of the murder." His eyes flicked to Sienna and then back to his screen. "Mila reported a Feral on the canal, but she closed the breach before anything else could come through."

"Where's Xander?"

"He's gone up to The Circus to deal with the wolves."

The door banged open. Perry stood in the doorway, his clothes burned full of holes, the scent of smoke on him. "Where do you need me, Bridget?"

She held up a hand to stop him, nodding to Jerod to continue.

"There are reports from Oxford as well as London. Multiple breach points."

"They're testing the defenses," Bridget said softly. "The canal is new. They haven't used water magic before. And so soon after Michael …" Her voice trailed off. "We can't wait any longer. We can't be on the defensive anymore." Bridget looked over at Perry and then to Sienna. "The new Extreme Cartographic Force must go into the Borderlands. We must have the Map of Shadows."

Sienna didn't understand why Bridget was looking at her in that way. She was overwhelmed by the things she had seen today; the existence of the Borderland and magic; her father's decision to leave her, and the possibility that he could still be alive. Her head reeled with it all.

And she was no Mapwalker – was she?

"Perry, take Sienna to the training room." Bridget's eyes narrowed. "We'll see what she can do."

Sienna took a step back. "No, I don't want this. My father and grandfather didn't even want me involved. I'm leaving."

She stared at Bridget with an unflinching gaze until the woman nodded.

"Go then, back to the map shop. But be aware, Sienna, there is no way you can escape this. The border is weakening, and if Bath falls, the rest of the country will follow. The maps will be rewritten and you may not have a choice in the days to come. Perry, escort Sienna back up to the Abbey level."

Perry turned, gesturing towards the door. "Let's go."

They walked back down the corridor as the sounds from the War Room faded behind them. Sienna felt an overwhelming sense of disappointment in herself and yet she wondered why. After all, she didn't ask for this. Perry walked by her side in companionable silence, but as they passed the room where he had been burning everything but the maps, he spoke.

"I know how you feel, Sienna, but Mapwalkers don't choose this life. We are born into it." He sighed. "Sometimes our parents are not the people we want them to be. Sometimes *we* are not the people we want to be. But if you're a Mapwalker, and Bridget believes you are, then I hope you might come with us into the Borderlands." He stopped and turned to her. Sienna looked up at his earnest face. "There are two sides, and we defend the border between them. Right now, we need all the help we can get."

He led her back through the winding corridors up to the Abbey level and held the door open for her to leave. "I hope to see you again."

Sienna emerged into the sun in the heart of Bath. A tourist group of Koreans wandered into the square, their guide talking into a tiny microphone as the huddle looked up at the Abbey. Sienna turned with them, trying to see it again with new eyes. The church loomed over the city, its ancient walls hiding something she had never known was beneath. She supposed that she wouldn't even be able to get back down there again unless she decided to join them. The best thing to do was forget this ever happened.

She walked back up towards the map shop, but the police now barred the way toward The Circus. Through the cordon, up the road, she could see mist hanging in the air around the Georgian buildings, obscuring the trees. She wondered who Xander was and what he could possibly be doing with the beasts. A smile ticked at the corner of her mouth. How could she even be thinking about these things?

Sienna took a detour around the edge of Royal Victoria Park and up past the Marlborough pub, then walked back towards the map shop. Mila sat on the doorstep, a puddle of water around her as she dried herself in the sun, her face turned up to the bright rays. Zippy wasn't with her this time.

She opened her eyes at Sienna's approach, arching one perfect eyebrow. "I heard you turned Bridget down."

Sienna smiled. "Word travels fast. But I don't have any Mapwalking skills, so I don't know what I could do to help even if I wanted to."

She pulled the key to the shop from her pocket. Mila stood up. "I drowned a Feral this afternoon." Her voice sounded strangely disconnected. "He looked like a man, but he didn't exist on this side of the border, so perhaps he wasn't real at all."

Sienna didn't know what to say. Perhaps this was all some kind of weird joke to scare her off so she would sell the map shop. She thought of Sir Douglas Mercator. All she had to do was call him, and she could move to London and forget all this.

Mila put her hand on Sienna's arm. "This is real and you must be curious. What if you *can* mapwalk? What if you could see your father again? Come with me back to the canal boat, and I'll help you try."

Sienna looked around the shop. The maps whispered to her, speaking of dormant power and far-off places. She had spent too much of her life not knowing what she wanted, aimless and wandering. Maybe it was time to make her own map.

She turned back to Mila. "Okay, I'll come for coffee, and we'll give it a go. But if nothing happens, I'm selling the shop."

They walked up through the back streets and out onto the towpath at Bathwick, emerging by the side of the canal. It felt like a different world to the teeming city they had left behind. Their footsteps crunched along the gravel, and the sound of birdsong rang from hedgerows wound through with dog roses and elderflower. Violet irises grew in the reeds along the edge of the water and ducks swam along, skimming for bugs. The afternoon sun shone through the canopy of trees, dappling the path as they passed narrowboats moored on the bank.

"I never liked the city much," Mila said as they walked. "I grew up in London and escaped onto the canals when I could. Turns out I can mapwalk through waterways, which explains why I've always been so drawn to them."

They turned a corner to where a boat was moored. It was the green of spring leaves painted with a five-pointed compass alongside a map of the sinuous canal waterway dotted with trees and intricate birds. Zippy lay on the bank in a patch of sun, guarding the entrance. He saw them coming and ran to meet them, barking happily as he bounced up and down. Sienna couldn't help but smile at his enthusiasm and bent to rub his fur.

"You are a lovely boy. Yes, you are."

Mila laughed. "See why I have him? No matter how the day goes, no matter what craziness the world throws at me, I arrive home to this bundle of joy. Come in. I'll put the kettle on."

The boat rocked a little as Sienna stepped aboard. It was long and narrow inside, like a gypsy caravan. There was a tiny kitchen area right by the door, a little stove, and a bench top with a few mismatched mugs in different patterns. A small table next to a window looked out on one side to the path and on the other side to the canal itself. Two foldable chairs sat stacked against the side. Further back, there was a bookshelf, then a little sleeping cabin with a curtain across. It was a tiny self-contained world and Sienna could see that it had everything a person might need. Mila seemed to have her life pretty sorted.

Zippy ran down the middle of the boat and back again, twisting around their legs, wagging his tail, his little face alive with happiness. Mila laughed and opened out the chairs. Zippy immediately jumped up onto one of them. "Welcome to our humble abode."

"Do you move the boat a lot?" Sienna asked.

Mila shook her head. "Sometimes if I need to escape, but I like it here. We have quite a community on the canal. I have friends, people who love Zippy. We are the misfits up here. Sometimes Bath likes to forget we exist because most people on the canal don't have normal jobs. There are craftsmen, artists, some barely eking out a living doing odd jobs here and there. But I like being free. I can just untether myself from the bank and go if I want to. Not very fast, of course. It takes forever to get through the locks, especially if you're on your own, but I love it."

Mila put the kettle on and pointed to the chair. "Have a seat. I'll make us some tea and then show you how my Mapwalking works."

As Mila brewed and poured the tea, Sienna felt a nervous energy, her anticipation building. After taking a sip, Mila knelt down and pulled away a rug from the floor, revealing a tiny trapdoor underneath, lined with a waterproof seal.

"This is not normal on a narrowboat," she said with a laugh. "But I find it easier to travel this way because otherwise people would be questioning why I was jumping in and out the water all the time. This way I can slip in and out and no one knows about it."

Mila tugged open the trapdoor to reveal the canal water beneath. The smell of weeds and rushes rose from the hatch. "So, I mapwalk through waterways," she said. "It's hard to explain how to do it, but I sensed you felt a pull towards the maps in the shop. For me, the pull is towards water. I haven't seen myself traveling, of course, but it feels like I'm some kind of water creature because I don't have to come up to breathe. Like being in a ripple, moving in the spaces between the waves as they cross the water. It's not so much swimming, more like a direction with my mind. I've become better at it over time." She grinned. "First time I tried it I ended up in a weir getting rolled over and over by the flow, wondering if I could get out. But sometimes you just have to just try things."

Mila put her hand down into the water, and her skin rippled as if her flesh had become liquid.

Sienna gasped. "That's incredible."

"Call it magic." Mila shrugged. "Call it a different kind of human. Call it what you want, but I was born with this. Your family are known as powerful Mapwalkers, so perhaps you have something too." She pulled her arm out of the water and closed the hatch. "I'm not going to take you into the water today. We don't want you gasping and panting as you try and breathe underwater."

Sienna frowned. "Does that mean you can take other people when you mapwalk?"

Mila nodded. "Yes, as long as you're connected somehow. Holding hands or tied together or something. How many people you can take with you is entirely dependent on the level of your control and your power. I've only taken one other person before, but I heard your grandfather once rescued a whole group of people from a prisoner-of-war camp, transporting them out through a map. There are rumors of Mapwalkers like me helping boats through storms." Mila's eyes shone with excitement. "I like the idea of being some kind of superhero." Then she frowned. "But most of our work is about protecting the border and artifact retrieval these days."

"So how would I mapwalk?" Sienna asked.

"It's like giving in to a sensation," Mila said. "Your body knows what it wants to do. You were born for it, so you just have to let it do what it knows deep inside." She walked to the bookshelf and pulled out a map of Bath. She opened it on the table in front of Sienna. "This is a good start." She pointed to a place on the canal path. "We're here. There's The Circus. That's where the shop is. Why don't you start by using this map to get us back to the shop?"

"How?" Sienna's heart pounded. She felt like she was about to cross a line. Her father and grandfather had wanted her to stay away from this, but something inside made her desperate to try.

"Just put your hand on the map."

Sienna placed her fingertips onto the paper. An electric

sensation of vibration traveled through her skin. She pulled her hand away quickly.

"It's okay." Mila smiled with encouragement. "Just relax."

"What does it look like to someone watching?" Sienna asked.

"I've seen your grandfather travel, and he just disappeared," Mila said. "Whereas I shimmer as I go into the water. That's what Perry told me anyway. I think you met him."

Sienna smiled. "Yeah, fire boy."

Mila grinned. "You need to meet Xander as well. He's way too good-looking, but he can do some pretty interesting things with illustration. He has earth magic. He can form creatures and animals on the vellum of maps. If he draws it, it can become real."

Sienna frowned. "What type of magic does my family have?"

Mila went to the window and paused a moment before speaking. "Your grandfather and your father both had blood magic."

"That doesn't sound good."

"Well, it's a mixed blessing. It's the most powerful magic, used to create the original maps. You can draw a new map, or reinforce the borders, whereas the rest of us can only travel through existing ones. Blood Cartographers can remake reality."

Sienna laughed nervously. "Doesn't quite sound like me."

"Well, if nothing happens, then you don't have to worry about it. Just try thinking of the map shop. Visualize the lines of the city. Think of the whispers of the maps. Let them speak to you."

Sienna placed her hand back on the map. "Do I need to close my eyes?"

Mila smiled. "Whatever feels most natural. Just relax."

Sienna closed her eyes and concentrated on the sensation

of the map, the feel of the paper beneath her fingertips. She could almost sense each individual molecule in it. Then it was as if she rose above her body, a sensation of weightlessness, of almost flying. Suddenly she could see into the map like a 3D image of the city below.

The sense of vertigo overwhelmed her. She opened her eyes, gasping for breath.

Mila put a hand on her shoulder. "You're still here, but you were definitely flickering just then."

"It was like flying." Sienna's breath caught in her throat. She wanted to go back there. She wanted to try again. If this was what her father had felt, she knew why he had left his family to pursue this life. It was intoxicating. "I want to try again."

Mila nodded. "I'm coming with you." She put her hand over Sienna's.

Sienna closed her eyes again, letting the feeling flood through her, unresisting this time. She rose above the map, above the canal and concentrated on the map shop, zooming down in her mind, wishing herself there.

CHAPTER 7

"Open your eyes." Mila's voice was delighted.

Sienna opened them to find a tiny garden surrounded by a brick wall.

Mila laughed. "Where the hell are we?"

Sienna spun around. Then she looked up. "I think that's the back of the map shop. This is the garden I saw from the flat earlier."

Mila pulled out her smart phone. "These don't work in the Borderlands, but here they can be useful." She looked at the GPS. "We're just behind the map shop, so you almost got it right."

They laughed together. "Back to the canal boat then?"

Sienna grinned. "Sure, this is fun!" And it was. It made her heart sing, an exhilaration she had never experienced before.

She took Mila's hand, ready to mapwalk again, then realized there was no map to concentrate on. "The map's back in the boat? How do I travel through it?"

"That's why Blood Cartographers are so special. Most of us travel with our star maps to orientate us home and our own compasses. But if you can see the map in your head, you can travel it. For now, just think back to the picture of the map you have in your head and take us back to the canal boat."

Sienna closed her eyes and concentrated. She smelled the lavender of the gardens as they soared above the city and then they were back on the canal boat, falling about laughing as they drank their tea together.

"That was amazing. I want to try again," Sienna said. "Could I find my father like this?"

Mila frowned. "That's pretty advanced stuff. Your grandfather could find missing people, but it takes a lot of training. I don't think you should do it without supervision, without Bridget. She's also a Blood Cartographer. Let's just practice around Bath if you want to do it again. How about trying to get back to the Abbey?"

Sienna felt a rising buzz in anticipation. It was a rush and she wanted to feel like she was flying again.

She looked down at the map in front of her with the streets of Bath laid out in deliberate ways. She thought of all the maps back in the shop, a way to travel wherever she wanted. How could her father have kept this from her? How could he have wanted her to remain ignorant of this ability?

"I want to do it again." Sienna put her hand on the map, and Mila put her hand on top. Sienna closed her eyes. She thought about the stone interior of the Abbey, the huge blocks that made up the walls of the ancient place of worship. In her mind, she conjured up the sense of space above and beneath her feet, the gravestones of those who died a thousand years ago. Her father would have walked these streets too and traveled above them.

She pictured where the Abbey was, the roads surrounding the river and the canal. She could see the square outside and the ancient Roman Baths, the main shopping area and the little tea rooms where tourists sat eating Bath buns. Maybe her father had sat there too, thinking of her over the years.

But as she mapwalked, it felt different this time. An overwhelming sense of cold stone and death. There was a sense of flying, but this time it was as if she had crossed a shadowy threshold.

"Where are we?" Mila's voice broke through her concentration.

Sienna opened her eyes. The sense of coldness she had felt just a minute ago was real, and she shivered as the chill permeated through her thin top. It looked like a castle dungeon. Great blocks of stone made up the walls and stagnant water trickled down, stinking of sewers and rotting flesh, metallic blood and the stench of suffering.

A scream rang out, echoing through the rooms beyond.

Mila pulled Sienna against the wall, and they huddled, cowering, backs pressed against the stone. "This isn't the Abbey," Mila whispered. "I don't know where we are."

Footsteps padded past in the corridor outside. They stayed huddled against the wall waiting until the steps passed. The agonized scream came again, a sound of agony and torture. Sienna imagined what might be happening down here and her skin goose-bumped in fear.

It fell silent, and that was somehow worse.

Mila stepped away from the wall, her eyes wide as she looked around. "Oh, no." Her hand flew to her mouth.

Sienna gradually realized what hung around them on the walls. The place was hung with maps, but not of paper or vellum. The maps were of flayed human skin with map lines tattooed on them, etched into the flesh. The acrid smell of dried blood permeated the room. Sienna fell to her knees, gagging and coughing.

Mila knelt by her. "You have to be quiet," she whispered. "They might hear us. I don't know exactly where we are, but we're definitely in the Borderlands."

"What are these … things?" Sienna whispered as she gazed in horror at the gallery around them.

"Blood maps." Mila's eyes narrowed. "This is the dark side of your gift. Those with blood magic can create new places by etching maps with blood, and the most powerful method is to carve into human flesh. Each of the Blood Cartographers mark their skin over time, tattooing the places they care about most in order to protect them. Your grandfather, Michael, had The Circus and central Bath on his body. He protected the city with his blood." Mila frowned. "But the maps can be etched onto skin without permission. This is the work of the Shadow Cartographers."

Another scream rang out in the dungeon and Sienna had visions of someone strapped down as a knife carved lines of a map into warm flesh.

She understood now why her father wanted to keep her away from this world. Then a realization came to her. "Surely we can only be here if my father is here too? I was thinking about him as I began to mapwalk and this is where we ended up. What if he's here?" Sienna rose to her feet and went to the door. "I need to go and see."

Mila grabbed her arm, holding her back. "You can't go out there. The other side of being a Blood Cartographer is that *your* skin and *your* blood are the most powerful. If they mark you and skin you, they will have your power to remake maps." Mila pointed at the wall. "Do you want your flesh to hang here? Is this what your father would have wanted?"

Sienna sighed and stepped away from the door. Part of her was desperate to go and see whether it was her father screaming down the hall. But it was impossible. She shouldn't even hope that he was alive.

But she had to know for sure. She would go back to Bridget and join the Extreme Cartographic Force.

"We have to get back." Mila walked further into the room. "But before we go, we need to see what they have here."

Sienna looked more closely at one of the skin maps on the wall, her nostrils flaring at the fetid stench. The skin was from a woman, part of her breasts clearly visible, her legs hanging down like some disembodied jumpsuit. The skin had been tattooed with dark lines in black, marking out territory.

Mila leaned closer and then pointed her finger at a whorl-like shape. "This is the symbol for a mine, but it's a new minefield, for minerals or maybe coal or other kind of power generation. It's not a map to change the borders Earth-side. It's creating a new part of the Borderlands." She frowned. "They need power, so they need to mine, and if they can't go back over into Earth-side to get it, then they have to create it here."

Sienna took out her smart phone from her pocket to take some pictures but the screen was black, inert.

Mila looked over. "Technology doesn't work over here. Something about the way they created the border in the first place renders it unusable. Like a safety switch added to tip the balance in favor of Earth-side, I guess."

They walked around the room looking at the other maps tattooed on different shaped bodies. Some were still red and raw with droplets of blood dried in the lines of hills and cities. Some were older, more tanned, like an animal hide. And that is exactly what we are, Sienna thought. Just animals, in the end, our flesh rotted away, our skin merely leather. She shook her head at such a macabre thought.

Mila walked into the shadowed corner of the dungeon. "A five-pointed compass." Mila's voice was weak, her dark skin suddenly paler in the weak dungeon light. "It's only used by Mapwalkers. Each of us has a different compass rose, but all with five points. This one marks one of the last Extreme Cartographic Force, a woman who left with your father."

Sienna thought back to the picture on the wall, the team who were with him when he disappeared. "We have to check the rest of the bodies." Her voice was calm, cold as the air in the dungeon, but her skin prickled in anticipation for what they might find.

Was he hanging here?

They walked around slowly checking each of the hanging skins, but her father's wasn't there. Sienna exhaled sharply, relief flooding through her.

Then she noticed a small wooden door at the end of the dungeon. Sienna walked towards it and pushed it open. It creaked a little and she froze at the noise echoing through the dungeon.

But nobody came.

She walked inside, Mila close behind. A few oil lamps lit the room, casting red light around the walls. They were papered with maps of Earth-side, similar to those Sienna had seen in the library of the Illuminated Cartographer.

There was a huge map of Bath on one wall, with the Abbey in the center. Areas of the city had been stuck through with nails, hammered into the map next to razor slashes cut through streets. Burned houses had matches dug through them, smeared with soot. A small knife had been stuck into the heart of the Ministry, marking the site with blood.

"A fetish map," Mila whispered. "Blood Cartographers can change the shape of the world, but Bath is so well protected that they can't just destroy it and recreate it. But they *can* use a fetish map to bring pain and destruction to the city."

They looked around at the other maps on the wall. London, Jerusalem, Rome, and in the corner, Aleppo. The ancient city in Syria was littered with fetish marks, whole areas scratched out with razor blades and burnt matches thrust into ancient sites.

"Most of Old Aleppo is already in the Borderlands," Mila said softly. "Cities that are abandoned by so many, left in ruins, often are. Those who loved it enough to stay are either dead or forgotten and are pushed over into the Borderlands. This is why so many here are traumatized by war and disaster." Mila indicated the maps around them. "These maps are all cities with Ministry headquarters. Ancient places where the border has always been permeable, where it's easier to cross over." She turned back to the fetish map. "Whoever controls this map is planning on releasing hell into the city."

She reached out to pull it from the wall.

As she touched it, shouts rang out. The sound of feet running in their direction. Then another scream from down the hall.

Mila looked at Sienna. "We have to get out of here. There's no watercourse, so I can't do it myself. You have to do it."

They held hands and Sienna closed her eyes, desperately concentrating, trying to bring the image of the canal boat back to her mind. But the sound of screaming echoed through the dungeon, filling her mind with pain. She couldn't seem to lift herself into that three-dimensional world, out of her body, above wherever they were.

Mila pushed the door shut quietly, her eyes wide with fear. "It has to be now, Sienna. We don't have much time."

From outside the room, they heard footsteps enter into the hall of blood maps.

"They're almost here," Mila whispered. "Think of the map shop, think of your grandfather."

CHAPTER 8

HEART POUNDING, SIENNA THOUGHT of the map shop, the pedestrian street that ran in front of it, the maps whispering inside, their texture on her skin. There was a whisper of breath on her cheek, and the sounds changed as the dungeon faded. Cool stone disappeared, and she opened her eyes to find them both back in the shop.

"That was close." Mila uncurled her hand from Sienna's. "We have to go down to the Ministry and tell Bridget what we saw. And what you can do."

Sienna suddenly felt dizzy and sat down on the chair by her grandfather's desk, her head in her hands. "What *can* I do?"

"You don't need to have a physical map or know it by heart to mapwalk. I've heard rumors of that kind of magic, but it's incredibly rare."

Sienna looked up at her. "But I don't know how to do it again. It was a fluke, and you realize that we almost got ourselves killed, right."

Mila grinned. "But we're still here. You got us back."

"But not whoever was in that dungeon." The memory of the screams rang around Sienna's mind. "We have to get back there."

Mila raised an eyebrow. "Does that mean you're joining us?"

Sienna met her gaze and nodded. "If there's a chance that my father is alive, I've got to try and find him."

They left the shop and walked down towards The Circus again. The mist still shrouded the trees in the center of the round, but it faded even as they watched. Police stood guard, turning people away, but Mila walked towards them. As she approached, they lifted the tape.

"Afternoon, Miss Wendell," one said with a respectful nod.

"Afternoon, Constable." Mila ducked under the tape and Sienna followed, curious as to what they might find within the mist.

"The Ministry has close links with the local police," Mila explained. "Sometimes they pick up Ferals who make it across, or there are incidents with Borderland creatures. Most of them think we operate some kind of weird zoo."

They approached the perimeter of the mist and stepped through. Bath faded around them, and Sienna felt a sudden sense of expansive space, far bigger than was possible in the tiny circle. It had the same darker vibration that she had felt in the dungeon, the touch of the Borderlands. But it was faint, further away now.

A roar came from deep within the mist.

"What the –?" Sienna's words were cut off as a huge lion padded towards them, its golden mane thick, keen eyes fixed upon them. Its huge powerful shoulders rippled with muscle and the fur around its mouth was stained with blood. It bared its teeth.

Sienna froze.

"Just stay still," Mila whispered.

The lion came closer and sniffed at Sienna's clothes. Then it purred like a big cat and rubbed its head against her, almost knocking her over.

"He likes you." A young man stepped out from behind a tree. His hair was a dark mop of loose curls, and his languid demeanor suggested that he'd just woken up from some debauched party. A few days of stubble highlighted his jawline and full mouth, and his eyes were a bright hazel-green. Mist swirled around him as he walked towards them, his gait confident and in control.

Mila introduced them. "Xander Temple, meet Sienna Farren. Hopefully our newest Mapwalker recruit."

Xander walked closer, his eyes appraising. Then he grinned and reached out his hand to shake hers. "Good to meet you, Sienna. We could use someone new to keep Mila out of trouble."

Mila nudged him in the ribs and they both laughed. Xander bent to kneel on the ground and wrapped his arms around the lion's neck, leaning his head against the soft fur. "This big softie is Asada. We've just been finishing off the last of the Ferals, and the border is now closed again."

He was so close to the powerful blood-stained jaws but there was no fear in Xander's eyes. Sienna noticed flecks of gold there, echoing the creature's golden gaze.

"You walk around Bath with a lion?" she asked.

Xander stood and pulled out a tattered map of the city on a scrap of leather from his pocket. The edges of the map were inked with creatures, a tentacled sea monster and a shark in one corner, a dragon in the opposite, a coiled serpent and then a space in the top right where it looked like something was missing.

"I'm an Illustrator," Xander explained. "On every map, there are decorative cartouches, and the corners of maps often feature monsters, demons and animals. Illustrators have earth magic. We draw creatures, and they live." He petted the lion once more and then placed the map on the ground. Asada stepped onto it, and for a moment, it looked as if his heavy body would tear through. Then he disappeared, and the inked image of a lion appeared in the previously empty corner. Sienna blinked in surprise, but the lion really had gone.

Xander picked up the map and folded it neatly before putting it back in his pocket. "We all have our different gifts." He smiled. "But I have the coolest."

Mila snorted. "You wish."

The mist dissipated around them and the outline of the Georgian buildings appeared through the haze. A ray of sunlight burst through, turning the leaves a brilliant green as a gust of wind made them rustle. The Circus was back to its usual self again.

Sienna's anticipation grew as the three of them walked down the hill back towards the Abbey. In a single day, the direction of her life had changed beyond recognition. By stepping back into the Ministry, by actively choosing to return with Mila and Xander, she was taking it even further – and she was ready for it.

As horrific as that dungeon had been, something had called to her there, something dark within her echoed to the heartbeat of the Borderlands. She craved that feeling again, but she needed backup next time. At least until she learned how to use her Mapwalking skills and could go alone.

They arrived back at the Ministry door, and this time, Sienna felt more at home. With Mila and Xander by her side, she could face Bridget.

They walked down the long corridor towards the War Room. Bridget stood looking at charts while Perry was deep in conversation with one of the other men. Bridget looked up as they entered, a smile dawning on her face.

"I'm glad you came back, Sienna."

Mila explained what they had seen in the dungeon within the Borderlands. Bridget's eyes widened at the five-pointed compass on one of the skins.

"Are you sure that's what it looked like?"

Mila nodded.

"Then it was Jenny, part of your father's team, Sienna. She was an Illustrator."

Xander turned away, cursing under his breath.

"The fetish map you saw is a version of our world twisted into something darker. It is not real yet – but it could be. Was there anything else that might help you get back there?"

Mila shook her head.

Bridget thought for a moment. "There might be something. Mila, help Perry and Xander prepare for the mission. Sienna, follow me."

They walked together back up the corridor to the wooden door marked Blood Gallery. Bridget stopped outside.

"Blood maps are part of Mapwalker heritage. Each Blood Cartographer tattoos themselves over a lifetime of magic. The tattooing is part ritual, part protecting that which we love." She rolled up the sleeve of her shirt to reveal a tattoo of Dublin, the lines of the port and the River Liffey, marks for the castle and the cathedral. Her eyes softened as she looked at Sienna. "Your grandfather tattooed these for me."

Bridget unlocked the door. "When a Blood Cartographer dies, their skin is kept as a powerful map. It might seem macabre, but the layers of blood and tattoos over generations have kept the border sealed and safe."

She pushed open the door. A cool blast of air rushed out and Sienna's skin goose-bumped in response. Bridget stepped inside. "Follow me."

Like the dungeon, this gallery was hung with skins, but they were displayed with respect here, rather than roughly nailed to the walls. Each was framed with the name of the dead inscribed beneath it, and a portrait or a photo of the Cartographer alongside their five-pointed compass rose. It smelled of tanned leather, of a museum, not of death. But the skins were the same macabre items they had seen in the dungeon.

"This is one of the oldest Blood Galleries," Bridget explained, "although there is one in every major Ministry location around the world. Each Blood Cartographer understands that this is where we will end up. Part of our responsibility is tattooing while we're alive in order to seal the borders with our blood."

Sienna shivered as she looked around at the skins. "So what were the skins we saw in the Borderlands?"

Bridget frowned. "They would have been forcibly tattooed. Jenny was only an Illustrator, her magic wasn't strong, but the Shadow Cartographers could have used her skin to inscribe with blood and pervert what we have done as a sacred rite for generations."

"Who are they?" Sienna whispered.

"Think of the border as the line between light and dark," Bridget explained. "Those who operate beyond it are known as Shadow Cartographers. They have the same magic as us, but it's stronger over there. It gets even more powerful the further out they go, beyond the Borderlands into the Uncharted." She turned and indicated the skins. "But we have the numbers. There are still more of us than them … for now, at least."

"So why can't you just take control? Why are there so many incursions over the border?"

Bridget sighed. "Political events have tipped the balance in recent years. There are more people than ever pushed forcibly over the border, and they remember what it was like over here. Those people want to get home. But the border has been porous one way for generations, and only Mapwalkers have been able to cross both ways. Now we've heard that this Map of Shadows will remake the border in their favor."

"What will that mean?" Sienna asked. "I'm still not clear on how the border works."

Bridget smiled. "It's not like a hard border, patrolled by men with guns and dogs, where you need to present a passport to cross. Think of it more like a river, which acts as an ever-moving flow. When you cross it, you might enter at one point and emerge at another. And it can alter the banks on either side over time."

Bridget walked further into the room, stopping at one of the older skins set behind glass in a temperature-controlled environment. "This is a good example." She pointed at the lines, a group of islands off the eastern coast of Canada. "This is Newfoundland, and this is the Isle of Demons, which first appeared on maps in the sixteenth century, tattooed by one of the new world blood mages back then. But it disappeared in the mid-seventeenth century, and it's now part of the Borderlands. No one cared enough to keep it this side, so the darkness encroached and took it over."

Bridget turned, her eyes serious. "This could happen to Bath. This could happen to anywhere Earth-side."

"Why do the Shadow Cartographers want this land so much?" Sienna asked.

"Think about an olive tree planted in the soil that exists in the same place for a thousand years. The descendants of the original owner still think it belongs to them, but in later generations, as time passes and the man moves away, new owners come and resettle the land. The descendants of the new owners think it belongs to them too. There are many in the Borderlands who believe that Earth-side is still their home. But time moves differently over there and what they left behind often doesn't exist anymore."

"But who's to say which side is right?" Sienna asked.

Bridget smiled. "This is why you're meant to be with us. You see things differently because you haven't been brought up as a Mapwalker. Our mission is always to protect the border, to retain Earth-side as it has always been."

The door opened and Mila walked in, followed by Xander and Perry. Bridget turned to the four of them. "We don't have time to train you any further. Bath has the most ancient gate and the most well-fortified. If the border breaks here, England may fall. Make no mistake about it. We are at war. Some of you have seen what happens to slaves at the edges of the Borderlands. That could be our fate if you do not find the Map of Shadows."

Xander slouched against the doorframe. "No offense to Sienna, but why is she involved in this? She doesn't even know what ability she has."

He looked over at her and shrugged an apology. Sienna smiled back. "Oh, I understand. I didn't even know about this place until today, and now you're telling me I'm going into the Borderlands to find something I don't know anything about. It seems pretty crazy to me too."

Bridget raised a hand to silence them. "Mila mapwalked with Sienna today to a castle at the heart of the Borderlands. I've heard of it but never found it even though I looked, and I've ranged the Borderlands for twenty-five years. There is something that links Sienna to that dungeon, and the Blood Gallery suggests they might be creating the new map there, so you will need her. Your mission is to find the Map of Shadows and bring it back to the Ministry so the fire mages can burn it. Then we can re-strengthen the Border before it is weakened so much that the edges are frayed for ever."

"Why can't you come with us?" Sienna's voice was soft.

"I …" Bridget paused, her eyes full of regret and Sienna sensed she was hiding something. Then her voice hardened.

"It is your time. Your star charts overlap at this point in history. We have seen this conflict coming for many years, and we knew this day would come. Of course, we had hoped to prevent it. That's why the last Extreme Cartographic Force went over. But the prophecy speaks of the children of powerful mages coming together to defeat the shadow. The Illuminated Cartographer saw you would come, Sienna." Bridget shook her head. "I have been the one with unbelief. But now we don't have much time. You need to follow the footsteps of the last Force."

"Why doesn't Sienna just mapwalk us back to this basement dungeon?" Perry asked. "Surely that would get us closer to where we need to be."

"I don't know how to get back there," Sienna said, acutely aware of how inadequate her ability was. "I don't even know how I did it the first time."

"Go easy on her," Mila said. "Remember how it was starting out for all of us."

Bridget nodded. "I know you're not a team yet, and if we had all the time in the world I would take you out into the Cotswolds, train you, build you into a team as I did with the last Force. But we don't have time now. I have to trust you will find it in yourselves to look after each other. This is your home. All of you stand to lose something if the Borderland bleeds through, and if the Shadow Cartographers take the Ministry..." Bridget trailed off, and in her silence, Sienna sensed what might happen, how the skins in the dungeon were created and what fate might await them if they failed.

"So how are we meant to find it?" Perry asked. "If you weren't able to locate the castle, how are we meant to?"

"There are many ways into the Borderlands, and you will go in through the same map the last Force went through, a map that has the power to take you deeper into the Borderlands than any other, a map that has been protected for a thousand years."

CHAPTER 9

THE NEXT MORNING SIENNA rose early, excited to be off on the mission, anticipation rising within her. She had spent the night in her grandfather's flat. Although technically it was her flat now, she couldn't yet think of it that way. She had lain awake thinking of him last night, how she wished that she had got to know him while he was alive, but there was no time for regret now. She had eventually fallen asleep, dreaming of flayed skin and beasts from the edge of the map.

As she ate her breakfast, Sienna leafed through some of the journals, looking for anything that might mention a dungeon, a castle, anything her grandfather had written about the Borderlands. But the books were mostly sketches of what he had seen, strange enough, but nothing obvious to help them now. Did her father keep journals like this, and where might they be?

The bell rang, interrupting her thoughts. Sienna opened the door to find Mila standing outside, two takeaway coffees in her hands.

"Thanks. That's exactly what I need." Sienna smiled and took one. She indicated her small bag. "I've brought everything I have. It's not much. I didn't expect to stay long."

Mila laughed. "Don't worry, we have everything we need

in the military packs we take with us. There are also dead drops where we leave equipment, weapons, rations and other things over the border." She grinned. "I might also have some extra stashes the boys don't know about."

She pulled a small rolled-up leather map from her bag. "But you should keep this with you. It's your star chart. Just in case."

Sienna took it and put it deep within her pack as a horn beeped from the end of the road. Perry sat at the wheel of a four-wheel drive, Xander in the front next to him.

"Come on, you two," Perry called out. "We need to get going. Hereford awaits."

"Hereford was once Welsh," Xander said, as they drove out of town. "The border has changed multiple times. An early charter from 1189 had Hereford situated in Wales, as granted by Richard the First of England. But now it's English."

"And proudly so," Perry said in his impeccable accent, keeping his eyes on the road.

Sienna felt a little out of place in the car. She was an outsider but the other three didn't seem like a well-honed team either. They were more like a group of students going to a festival together. Xander turned up the radio as they headed west over the Severn Bridge and north through Wales. It wasn't long before they arrived in Hereford and pulled up near the cathedral.

Sienna looked up at the twelfth-century Romanesque church. "It's gorgeous."

Perry stretched as he got out of the car. "This was the Saxon capital of West Mercia in the eighth century, then the Welsh targeted the city in the eleventh century supported by the Vikings. There was once a castle here as big as Windsor in size and scale. The Welsh attacks were repelled, and it became a stronghold for the campaigns of English kings during the Welsh Marches. Pretty cool."

They walked towards the cathedral.

"We need to find a specific book in the chained library," Mila said. "Your father and his team came here before they went missing, Sienna."

"Sometimes I think a missing father might be better than any father at all," Perry muttered under his breath.

They walked into the cathedral and looked up at the decorative Norman columns and arches. Stone tombs with effigies of knights stood in alcoves off the nave and at the south end, there was a Norman font large enough to immerse a child. Knights Templar in chainmail armor decorated one of the tombs. The Bishop buried inside had been a Grand Master long ago. Underneath their feet were markers of the dead, those buried here for years, their bones resting under the flagstones, carved names fading under the footsteps of the faithful.

They walked past the choir, and Mila pointed to a bare patch on the wall. "The Mappa Mundi hung here for many years, but now it's kept safe in a separate building. That's what we're here to see."

"As well as the chained library," Perry said. "The Extreme Cartographic Force used the Mappa Mundi to travel through, but it's big, and we need to know which part. There are many entrances to the Borderlands, and we need to make sure we take the right one."

They walked out of the church to the special center where the library and the map were held.

"Mappa Mundi means map of the world," Mila explained, as they walked across the forecourt. "It dates to around 1300AD and gives a view of how the medieval monks understood the world back then."

They entered the temperature-controlled room to find the Mappa Mundi lit with dim lights behind glass. Sienna walked closer to get a better look. It was truly incredible, a single piece of vellum illustrated by the hand of faith, with representations of myth and legend next to places that really existed. Perhaps this was the truth of maps. In part, they reflected the world as it actually was, and in part, they reflected the way the world could be, or as it was imagined. As Sienna looked at the Mappa Mundi, she began to understand why her father had gone on this quest.

At the very top, an enthroned Christ held his hands up to show the stigmata, the wounds of crucifixion. Next to him, believers rose from their graves and entered Heaven, while on the other side the damned were stripped, chained and dragged down to Hell where a great beast waited to devour them. Sienna shivered as she looked at the creature, imagining an Illustrator like Xander drawing it and calling it into existence. She looked over at his handsome profile. Was it possible that he and others like him could create something so terrible?

Sienna turned back to the map. An inaccessible circular island at the top of the world represented Eden, surrounded by a ring of fire and closed gates. A serpent waited while Eve held out her hand to accept the apple, ready to taste the fruit of the knowledge of good and evil. Sienna understood her temptation, her need to know, because that's just how she felt about the Borderlands right now.

There was a picture of Noah's Ark, the woven hull floating above a sea of red when God sent the great flood to wipe out the wickedness of humanity. The map showed a path through the Red Sea, the color still fresh after so many years, marking the wanderings of the Israelites from Egypt, out of slavery and into the Promised Land.

There were beasts on the map, a unicorn, a lynx slinking towards the southern coast of the Black Sea, a war elephant with a tower on its back, a strange parrot creature with a curled tail. There were strange-looking people too: a man with no head, only eyes on his chest holding a sword, another with one huge foot. There were troglodytes, cave dwellers in Africa, and men with heads of dogs.

"What is this map about?" Sienna asked. "It can't be real, surely?"

"A map is never truly real," Mila said. "It's only one aspect of the reality of the creator. But we need to pay attention to the cities on the map. Maybe your father took the Force through one of those?"

Hereford was marked by a tiny building on the River Wye, almost rubbed off by pilgrims touching it over the years. Jerusalem was right in the center of the map, with a circular wall and a castle city with eight towers, marking the place of crucifixion.

Rome was shown as a towering cathedral with text next to it: 'Rome, head of the world, holds the bridle of the spherical earth.' Towers and pinnacles marked Paris, where the medieval University focused on philosophy and theology.

"The map is apparently a single piece of calfskin, but I think it's something different." Xander bent as close as he could get without the alarms going off. The map was drawn on the flesh side of the skin, not the hair side, making the map undulate as one was naturally more taut than the other. "I think it's the skin of an animal from the Borderlands. There's a vibration from it as if it calls to go home. Maybe something wandered over back then, but it's certainly more than just calfskin from Earth-side."

A labyrinth caught Sienna's eye, a circular maze, like the one in Crete with the Minotaur at the center. In the Middle Ages, many medieval cathedrals had labyrinths and pilgrims would walk around them looking for a way to the center, metaphorically searching for a way to God. She had visited Chartres Cathedral with her father years ago and they had walked the famous labyrinth together.

Mila pointed to a particular area of the map. "This is the camp of Alexander the Great. His conquest of the Persian Empire and domination of the known world was a popular theme, and there are several references on the map about

Alexander. This restraining wall was built to save the world from the destructive force of the Sons of Cain." She turned to Sienna. "Does anything here seem familiar?"

Sienna stared at the map, trying to see it with her father's eyes, trying to understand what he might have seen. He had traveled to many of the places portrayed but her eyes kept being drawn back to the labyrinth. "I'm not sure. Maybe we should look at the chained library. We can come back and check the map afterwards."

They walked through into the largest surviving chained library in the world. A librarian stood talking to a tourist group in front of them. "There are over 1500 books in the library and several hundred medieval manuscripts. There has been a library here since the year 800, and people still come from all over the world to examine them."

As the tourist group moved on, the librarian nodded in welcome, greeting the little group and then indicating the stacks. "Our most popular works are the Hereford Gospels, the Hereford Breviary and the sermons of St Bede."

She opened one of the books chained to a wooden lectern. "As you can see, there are miniature paintings and incredible illumination around the edges of many of the books. They were chained for their security, as there weren't very many books back in those days. We keep a few like this for historical accuracy." They walked through to the Hereford Gospels. "This is possibly the earliest surviving book made in Wales containing all four Gospels. It survived the sacking of the cathedral, and is revered as a relic for making it through the fire and destruction."

"Do you have any more illustrated books?" Xander asked.

The librarian nodded. "The Nuremberg Chronicle is one of the largest and most lavishly illustrated of the books dating from the fifteenth century. It tells the history of the world and has nearly two thousand woodcut illustrations."

Mila stepped forward. "Do you have a list of people who have visited and what they looked at?"

The librarian frowned. "Of course, but it's private information."

As she walked away, Mila turned to the others. "We need to come back later, after dark, so we can access those records."

* * *

It was after midnight when they crept back into the grounds of Hereford Cathedral, skirting around security lights and heading straight back to the library. Mila took a tiny piece of map parchment from her pocket and poured some water from a bottle over it. She laid it over the electronic locks and then used her magic to freeze it, cracking the locks from the inside. Sienna smiled. "Nice skill."

Mila grinned. "We all have our tricks." She looked over at Perry. "And it's less damaging than fire."

Inside, the library was quiet, and the four of them went straight to the librarian's station. Perry sat down at the computer. "I'm not all flames and fire, you know." He began tapping at the keyboard, looking for a way into the databases.

Sienna and Mila concentrated on the pile of old visitor books stacked in rows behind the desk. Xander stood watching for a moment, his eyes darting to the next room. "I think I'll go have a look at the Nuremberg Chronicle while we're here."

Mila raised an eyebrow as he walked off. "Xander is obsessed with illustrations."

The visitor books dated back over the last thirty years, so they pulled the older ones down first, flicking through the pages. It was strange to see the handwriting of people who'd visited many years ago. How many of them had passed on now? How many had found what they were looking for, and how many more had discovered new questions?

"Come and look at this," Perry said suddenly, his voice excited. Sienna and Mila went to stand behind him.

"Look, there was a break-in reported around the time the Force crossed over. They must have accessed the map then."

"But we still don't know which part they used to travel through," Mila said. "At least it gives us a narrower window to check the archives."

They turned back to the visitor books, pulling down one after the other.

Then Sienna saw her father's writing on the page, his distinctive sloped letters in purple ink. She touched the words with gentle fingers, thinking of him standing here in the library, a frown on his face as he concentrated. Did he think of her at all? She shook her head. She could only hope there would be time to ask him.

"He requested *Meditations on a Medieval Labyrinth*, so they must have gone through the labyrinth part of the map."

"Then that's the way we'll follow," Mila said. "Are you ready?"

Sienna nodded. "You put the books back, and I'll get Xander."

She left Mila re-stacking the shelves and walked through the library into the next room. Xander stood by a window, the light of the moon touching the book lying on the desk in front of him. It was chained to the wooden lectern, and she could see the detailed illustrations from across the room, the colors still bright after so many years. Xander sketched a dragon, a beast of scales and teeth and power, into the pocket journal he held. It was fat with extra notes and pages, and Sienna could only imagine what he drew in there, the creatures he held in his mind.

Xander looked up at her footsteps, his face taut with concern, then relaxing as he saw it was her. He indicated the page. "I've always wanted to illustrate a dragon, but Bridget asked where we'd put it and how we would hide it from the city." He shook his head with a sigh. "Such mundane questions when we should be using our abilities to the full, not hiding them."

Sienna walked closer and looked at the intricate lines on the page. "How do you create them?"

"The creatures can't come alive on any paper. I have to draw them on the edges of existing maps, preferably vellum or leather. I can't create maps from nothing as you can."

Sienna shrugged. "As I *supposedly* can. I haven't actually created a map yet."

Xander closed the book, his hand touching it lightly with respect. "The most powerful Illustrators have always worked closely with Blood Cartographers. Perhaps we could –"

Footsteps came from the corridor behind them, cutting off his words. Mila poked her head around the doorway.

"Come on, you two. Time to get going."

The four of them walked back to the Mappa Mundi, which lay within its protective case. Mila froze one of the panes of glass and made a hole big enough for Sienna to reach in and touch the map.

She hesitated, her heart beating faster. "So what do I do again?"

Mila took her hand. "Put your fingertips over the labyrinth and fix the image of it in your mind. Just think of the Borderlands as a country with multiple ways in. This map is one of the doors, but it should be where the last Force went through and then we'll try to pick up their trail on the other side."

Sienna nodded. "And you can all come through with me?"

"We'll link hands," Perry said. "But it's a bit like a gate. You're opening it, and then we can come through after you. We're all Mapwalkers, remember that."

"I just don't want to leave anyone behind."

Perry smiled. "It's okay. We're coming too. We're not missing out on this adventure."

Sienna put her hand through the hole and touched the smooth skin of the map. It had a vibration under her fingers, a certain texture. She sensed that, as Xander had thought, it was not of Earth-side, but from the Borderlands originally. A creature that had once existed on the other side had somehow come through here, slaughtered away from its home and now revered as part of history.

Sienna placed her fingertips over the labyrinth and held out her other hand. The three others put their hands over hers, and Sienna closed her eyes, letting the sensation of lifting take her up and out of herself, over the city of Hereford. Spreading below her was the skin of the world with Jerusalem shining like a beacon further out on the horizon, but below her, she could see a form of the labyrinth. It called to her, and she dived back down into it.

CHAPTER 10

SIENNA OPENED HER EYES.

It was dark, but the air smelled different. Whereas the inside of the library had a sense of dust from the pages of old books, the air here smelled of smoke and ash. Sienna looked around.

They stood on a street, hemmed in on all sides by shelled-out buildings, towering close and dog-legging away so she couldn't see very far. It was a warren of narrow streets, not even big enough for a car to drive down, an urban labyrinth. Empty rooms looked down on them like vacant eyes, the stone crumbling, a place where nature had started to reclaim the emptiness.

"It's Old Aleppo," Mila said. "The part of the city pushed over the border."

Sienna felt the shadow as a visceral sense on this side. It was like a darkness pushed down inside her all her life, which had suddenly found its way to the surface. All the things she'd been told she couldn't have, or be, or do, suddenly welled up inside her like a rush.

A shadow rush.

She didn't have to be a good girl here. She could take what she wanted. She could *be* who she wanted. There seemed no limit on what was possible in the Borderlands. It was dizzying, intoxicating and Sienna felt the thrill of the dark side in her veins as they walked. A sense of losing control to a point but without having a drink, without taking drugs, without loosening the mind in a way she would have to do on Earth-side in order to feel this way.

Mila looked over with a half-smile on her face, recognition in her eyes. "That feeling is why the Ministry send us in teams. Because if you come over on your own, there's a chance you won't return. You could go native with the rush, and then you'd be lost."

"Have you ever been over on your own?" Sienna asked.

Mila raised an eyebrow. "What do you think?"

Sienna grinned. Together the four of them walked through the ruined city. It had the haunting echo of lives long forgotten, the beauty of decay inherent in the buildings left behind. Sienna glanced into one shattered space. The walls were a fresh orange color, and a blue frieze ran around the edges as if it had only been painted yesterday. But the doorframe was rotten and broken and the floor covered in sand and rocks blown in on a cruel wind.

Could there be any true beauty without the knowledge it would fade? Sienna thought of the flowers she sometimes took to her mother and how they were only fresh for a few days before dying. This place felt like that. Like it was once a blooming flower now fallen into decay. Entropy had taken it to dust, as it took us all eventually.

It started to rain. Sienna looked up at the dark clouds overhead. "How does the weather get here?"

Mila laughed. "The weather doesn't know the border, so the same rain falls on us and the Borderlanders alike. But natural events sometimes drive people over, like earthquakes and eruptions. Time is different the further out you go towards the Uncharted. There are still some out there who remember the destruction of Pompeii."

Sienna shook her head in amazement. It would be

fascinating to meet someone who had seen the eruption of Vesuvius, yet for them, it would have been the end of all they knew.

"How do you know what's here in the Borderlands?" she asked.

"It's a challenge as the edges are not entirely mapped," Mila said. "They move over time as people and places are driven off the edge of Earth-side. Those who are not wanted, who fall between the borders, find a place here. But, of course, there is a hierarchy between those who have been here the longest and those who arrive every day. There are refugees here too. Sometimes I think we are driving them over here on purpose." Mila sighed. "Sometimes I don't know which side we're on."

They walked down the cracked street under the arches of a ruined hall, the stone pockmarked by artillery shells. Sienna picked her way through the rubble, over fallen masonry and discarded furniture. There were signs of habitation in the rubble, a chipped cup and saucer, the tattered remains of a book, the springs of a bed frame.

Suddenly, they heard shouting up ahead.

The four of them huddled in a doorway, sheltered by a broken wall. The sound of running feet came closer and then a group of men passed, their faces set in determination, each with a half-moon tattoo.

"They have people here who can sense the border opening," Mila whispered. "They're looking for us."

After the men passed by, the group walked on with light feet, staying alert in the shadows. The smell of smoke from a fire wafted from a doorway and Sienna stopped to peek inside. A man lay on the ground, his face thin and drawn with pain, his limbs curled. A woman knelt by the fire boiling water in an old tin can, a baby next to her in the dust, a blanket wrapped around its thin body. The woman looked up with fearful eyes.

Sienna saw just another human there, someone who wanted to look after her family, someone who wanted to stay alive. She could understand why those in the Borderlands wanted to come back over to Earth-side. This place had been pushed out because nobody cared. The powers that be made their maps and decided what was important, *who* was important. The rest disappeared over here, cast adrift to survive alone.

The sound of shouting came from up ahead, deep voices raised, orders given. The woman turned back to the fire, not even flinching at the noise. Sienna walked on quickly after the others as they darted between alcoves in the buildings.

Perry turned around as she approached. "Try and keep up, we wouldn't want to lose you in here."

"Where are we heading?"

"The center of Old Aleppo. It's a souk, a trading market that stood for seven hundred years. At least it did stand until the war on Earth-side which now continues over here."

"Who's the fighting between here?" Sienna asked.

"The Borderlands are not just filled with one people," Perry said. "Factions fight each other for control of scarce resources." He stopped at a wall painted with a half-moon symbol in a dark ochre that could have been dried blood. "There are two factions in Old Aleppo. This symbol belongs to a warlord loyal to the Shadow Cartographers who sacrifices to the old gods. The price of human life is cheap Earth-side, but it's worth even less in the Borderlands. The Shadow Cartographers feed on the energy of violence, conflict and death, so they fan the flames to keep people in constant fear."

The stench of rotten flesh came on the air, a night breeze bringing it across the city. Sienna put her hand over her face, but they kept walking towards it, the smell intensifying.

"The warlord hangs the bodies of the rebels here," Perry said. "Around the labyrinth where the Resistance are known to be active."

The shadows shifted. Six bodies hung on the wall, hands tied behind their backs, hoods over their heads.

"We have contacts in the Resistance, those who trade for information. That's where we're going."

They walked past an abandoned temple. Holes in the roof let in shafts of moonlight. Sienna caught a glimpse of a mosaic on the back wall showing a god devouring his children.

Mila dropped back to walk next to her and pointed in at the statues of old gods. "Anything lost from Earth-side remains here in the shadows, including belief. There are people here who crawled over the border in the aftermath of ethnic cleansing. Those who escaped the massacres of Rwanda, of Srebrenica. The Borderlands claim those who would otherwise disappear on Earth-side." Mila shook her head.

"Is anyone born here?" Sienna asked.

Mila frowned. "Of course, there are children here, like anywhere. Some are Halbrasse, half-breeds. The Shadow Cartographers are trying to spawn a new generation of Mapwalkers, those who can cross the border like us. But to create such children, they risk creating abominations, those in whom magic twists into something that shouldn't live."

Sienna shivered. No wonder they needed to stop these people coming back over. For how could those on Earth-side stand against the inhumanity done here? The blood-soaked land did not forget what had been done to it, and the people who remained on the Borderland were the scars, the living tissue of what had gone before.

Mila stopped in front of the ruined building. "Things here are often not what they seem. You need to be careful. The Borderlands have a way of slipping inside you." She put her hand up, gesturing for them to stop and wait.

Sienna ducked into a doorway with Perry and Xander as Mila walked into the depths of the temple alone. The stones either side of the door were smashed, broken into pieces as if a gigantic hand had punched through them in anger. The thick beams stood out, charred and burned. It was a derelict skeleton, clouded with ash. Sienna looked down into the dust and noticed pieces of bone, shards of skull. They walked upon the bodies of the dead.

A few minutes later, Mila appeared at the broken door and beckoned them inside. Huge pillars dominated the space, rising to a roof that had been split asunder. A shaft of moonlight pierced down to the floor where carved spirals made the pattern of a labyrinth. There were sculptures in each of the alcoves around them, voluptuous goddesses with wreathes of dead flowers, the skeleton of a child in the lap of one. An offering to the dark goddess.

Mila stood with a tall man dressed in black leather. He turned at their approach.

"You didn't say you were bringing so many." His voice was deep and resonant. He stepped into a patch of moonlight and Sienna saw him more clearly. He had the regal bearing of an East African king, the limbs of a long-distance runner, the dark eyes of a moonless night. His head was closely shaved with stubble on his chin, highlighting a strong jaw.

"It's not safe here," he said. "We have to get moving."

Mila gestured towards him. "This is Finn Page. His father, Kosai, is the warlord here in Old Aleppo. Finn is the leader of the Resistance."

Finn turned to Mila. "If I do this, you'll keep your side of the bargain?"

She nodded.

"Then we must go now."

Finn led them out of the back of the temple, and they wound their way through the streets past the doorway that Sienna had glanced into before.

Finn turned around. "Wait here." He ducked into the room, and Sienna heard the rumble of his deep voice. He came back out a minute later, his face like thunder. "Follow me."

As Sienna walked past, she glanced into the room again. This time the woman had a loaf of bread, tearing at it hungrily as she shared it with her husband.

"My father has the relics with him tonight," Finn said, as they stalked through the ruined city. "The ritual is on the outskirts at the Tophet. We have a way to walk, then prepare yourself for Hell."

CHAPTER 11

SOMETIMES THE LANDLOCKED CITY was so hot that the air dragged through Finn's lungs with each breath and even though they were miles from water, it made him feel like he was drowning. Tonight was one of those nights, and the cloying stink of smoke from the pyres made it worse. He loosened his shirt at the neck, breathing more deeply, trying to push down the fear rising within him as he led the Mapwalkers deeper into the city.

Twisted metal lay in piles against sandbags covered in dust from destroyed buildings, the faint smell of buried corpses beneath. Trees grew in the rubble at the side of cracked roads, their leaves mottled black with disease but Finn heard the coo of a pigeon as they passed, evidence of life in the ruins. Soft voices came from one of the skeletal buildings behind it, scarred by the bombing he had only heard about. There were no guns in the Borderlands, although his father and his men spoke of them often, their voices lowered in remembrance of what they had lost during the wars that had devastated their native lands. Finn had been born here, a child of the Borderlands, so it was hard to know what was truth and what was myth in the stories they told.

He led the group into the ruins of the souk, the old market where a maze of market stalls had once stood. They followed him, footsteps echoing under the medieval stone roofs. He turned briefly to check on them, his eyes darting to the willowy young woman with titian hair. She was new, he sensed it in her curiosity, the way she couldn't stop looking around her even as she stumbled over loose bricks on the ground. There was an innocence about her, and Finn wondered what the city looked like through her eyes. She turned and looked at him. He felt a jolt inside, as if she saw right to his heart.

Finn walked on, but not before he realized that his father would want this young woman for himself. Her fragile Celtic beauty made her a prize, and he could trade her for sorely needed provisions. Together with the rest of the Mapwalkers, this group was worth a great deal, both to his father and to the Shadow Cartographers.

A worthy trade for his sister.

The young woman caught up to him, walking faster by his side. "I'm Sienna," she said, softly. "Can I ask what this place used to be?"

"The markets," Finn said, his voice gruff. "Spices, meat, vegetables, fruit. But now …" He shrugged. "We do what we can. In the daytime, people sell what they have grown and one day perhaps this place will be fully alive again."

Sienna smiled. "I hope so. I've been to the markets in Jerusalem – stalls piled high with peaches and pomegranates, the sweet smell of oranges in the air mingling with the yeast of freshly baked bread. Shoppers haggling for the best price and market traders calling out their best prices."

Finn smiled as her words brought back memories of happier times. "There are markets like those in the outer villages where they grow produce on the hills, even though the soil is poor. I go there to trade and bring back what I can."

"Can people who come over the border bring things with them?"

Finn frowned as he looked over at her. "You don't know?"

Mila caught up and took Sienna's arm, shooting her a

warning look. "Sorry, she's new on our team. I haven't fully briefed her yet."

Finn raised an eyebrow. Mila blushed, and the two dropped back to walk behind him, voices low. It was the first time he'd met a Mapwalker who hadn't been superior in both attitude and knowledge, someone with a real hunger to learn about this land.

His land.

Perhaps she would answer his questions about what life was like on Earth-side, a way to verify some of his father's more outlandish claims and what he had read in books. Because books did cross the border intact, unlike anything mechanical. Ancient magic kept out any technology created after the border was put in place, but books had become a form of currency, smuggled, traded, an addiction Finn had discovered early, even though the Shadow Cartographers banned them. He led the Mapwalkers on, weaving his way around the ruins, becoming lost in his own thoughts as he traversed the familiar path.

For all his father's faults, the warlord had always encouraged Finn and his other children to read. He even kept some of the forbidden books in his citadel at the heart of Old Aleppo, seized in raids or smuggled in across the border. The smugglers knew to stop at the citadel first, or their goods would likely be seized anyway. Kosai liked fine clothes and sold much of it on at a profit but always kept the best for himself. Some would be given to his family, the women he favored at the time, and of course, to his children.

His library contained works banned and banished on Earth-side, appearing in smoldering piles where they had been burned, popping through the border as their existence was denied. There were often intact volumes under the ash, their pages still readable.

But books also brought darker knowledge. His father's favorite was Suetonius' *Lives of the Caesars*, and descriptions of things done to those who crossed the Emperor now found their way into Kosai's court. His father drew his sense of justice from the examples of tyrants, determined to paint himself as a demigod, as the Roman Emperors had once done.

Kosai's faith had become stronger over time, and it had shown itself in the rule of fear. For those who doubt do not slaughter in the way that true believers do. Only those who believe in an absolute idea will kill in the name of it. It had been the Shadow Cartographers who showed Kosai the way of Moloch, resurrecting the ancient god so they could benefit from the fear he evoked.

There had been a time when Finn adored his father, when they had gone on father-son hunting trips into the forests at the edge of the Borderland towards the Uncharted to find the giant boars roaming there. As a six-year-old, his father had taught him to use a knife for the first time. Finn remembered the weight of it in his hand, a bigger knife than he could handle, but his father said heavy blades would help him learn faster. Finn put his hand down, touching the pommel of his sword in a reflexive movement. Those early years had been hard, but his father had taught him well.

Finn's mother had fallen through, brought here in a slave band and favored by the warlord for a time. She had died of an infection after the birth of another child and he scarcely remembered her face, although his skin color mirrored hers, rather than his father's Middle Eastern heritage.

Growing up, Finn hadn't paid much attention to his siblings, leading his own pack of young warlord princes. Together, they raided the outer towns, patrolling the edge of the border, waiting for new people to be pushed through, then enslaving them, selling them on. His father claimed these new arrivals were not real people, that they didn't have any rights here. They had been pushed out from their home, and thus were ripe to be exploited.

Isabel had been born when Finn was twelve, and he had never seen anyone so precious. He remembered holding her in his arms and promising he would never let anything happen to his little sister. Her blonde hair and fair skin were so different to his own, but the shape of their noses, the way they used their hands when they talked, and their love for books, bonded them.

Finn would read to her in the library, smuggling pocketfuls of dried dates in, so they could both nibble on the sweetness as they read passages aloud. He had taught her to read early on and he had taught her to use a knife as well. His father didn't believe in teaching the girls, but Finn couldn't see why his sister shouldn't be able to protect herself. As she had reached her teens, he'd seen the way men looked at her. And how Kosai had looked at her too.

Then one day, they came for her.

Finn lashed out, fighting away the guards until five of them held him down. Her screams echoed as they bundled her into the back of a wagon and took her away to the castle of the Shadow Cartographers.

The Resistance had come to Finn that night, as he walked through the streets of Old Aleppo down to the ancient library where he and Isabel had always found a haven. He paced in the darkness, thumping his fists against each other, unable to contain his anger. He decided to go after her, to track the wagon at first light, then bring her back or set her free.

He had heard what happened at the castle. There were women who had come back, their eyes hollow, their bodies broken from birthing children who might have some usable magic, the Halbrasse, the half-breeds.

Back then, a woman had stepped from the shadows. "I know what happened to your sister, but you can't stop them now. You will only die in your quest. There will only be more women taken, more children sacrificed. But if you stay, you have a chance to change things. Your father trusts you. You can be the eyes and ears of the Resistance inside his camp. If you hear of a raid, we can get there before you. If you hear of who will be targeted for sacrifice, we can spirit them away. And in time, we will help you save your sister."

"I need to know when," Finn said. "I can't leave her there, knowing what will happen to her every day."

The woman put a hand on his arm. "She is strong, as I was. I have told her how to end the life that might grow inside. There are pits outside the castle walls for the bodies of the children. The unborn or those who made it into the world briefly, those too mutated or too broken to live. Secrets written out of even this history. I knelt at the pit when I left that stinking place, I cried for the life I lost, but it gave me a purpose. And if you join us, we can end the Halbrasse for good." She met his eyes.

"The Resistance is working with Mapwalkers on Earthside. There are those who want to make peace across our borders, those who want to release the hold of the Shadow Cartographers. They want to help us build the Borderlands into a place where life is worth living. We just need to throw off the yoke of oppression."

Her words echoed inside Finn's heart. This was a quest worth joining, a cause worth championing. He couldn't be part of his father's bloody campaign any longer.

He nodded. "Tell me what you want me to do."

As Finn strode through the rubble of Old Aleppo, the team of Mapwalkers behind him, he remembered that night and the promise he would now fulfill. He was part of the Resistance, but he was going to get his sister, whatever it took.

CHAPTER 12

SIENNA TRIPPED ON A pile of rubble, cursing her clumsiness as she tried to catch up with the rangy Borderlander. Finn put his arm out to stop her falling, and she smiled up at him. "You said we were going to the Tophet. What is that?"

Finn's face darkened. "It's not something I would want you to see, but it's the only way to get to the relics." He met her eyes, and she saw anger there. "The gods pushed into the Borderlands demand blood, and the darkest rituals you Earth-siders banished now exist here. Chaos suits a certain type of person. Unfortunately one of those people is my father."

They walked out of the city, and the broken buildings soon gave way to the edge of a desert. The stars were high in the sky, and as Sienna looked up, she didn't recognize the constellations. It was a completely different view, as if the sky were inverted somehow. Finn led the way and as people passed on the road, many nodded at him, dipping their heads in respect.

Mila came back to walk beside Sienna. "Finn walks a fine line. Not for us, but for his people. He has respect as the son of his father, one of the most powerful warlords and certainly the most bloody. But now he works with the Resistance."

The sound of chanting came on a hot wind, a low rumble of voices repeating the name of a long-dead god.

They reached a sacred precinct, a circular area ringed with stones, topped with tiny skulls. At first, Sienna thought they might be animal bones. Some were so tiny that she could curl her fist around them. But as she looked closer, she realized they were babies and young children. A sense of foreboding filled her as they walked on.

In the center of the precinct, a crowd of people knelt in front of a large stone altar in the shape of the hungry god Moloch. His mouth was open to devour the sacrifice, and he held a basin of fire in his outstretched arms. The rhythmic chanting of the crowd grew stronger as a huge man walked forward, holding the wrist of a child of around four years old wearing a smiling mask.

"The mask hides their tears from the god," Mila said, her voice low.

The man dragged the child forward, and Sienna watched in rising horror, but they could do nothing as the place was surrounded by the warlord's men. They beat drums either side of the god to accompany the chants of the crowd.

"Why do the people allow this?" She looked up at Finn, shaking her head.

"They ask Moloch to grant them more than this life," he said. "They ask the god to break down the border. If you were trapped here in this hell, ruled by this tyrant, wouldn't you want that too? Besides, human sacrifice is a legacy from your Earth-side. Abraham was asked by God to sacrifice his own son, and in Homer's Iliad, King Agamemnon sacrifices his daughter Iphigenia for fair winds. Many of your ancient cultures had child sacrifice, and as it was banished, it ended up here."

Finn pointed around the back of the crowd. "This way. My father keeps the relics nearby, ready to be blessed with the fresh blood of the sacrifice. We have a little time before it's done."

They ducked down and ran around the edge of the crowd, keeping to the shadows amongst the grave markers.

A small temple stood out the back of the main complex. Two guards stood in front of it. They nodded their heads at Finn's approach.

"Stand aside," he said. "My father wishes me to take these pilgrims to the relics."

One of the guards looked confused. "I'm sorry, my Lord, but your father said not to let anyone in here tonight."

Finn stepped forward, pulling back his cloak to reveal a long sword at his side, the blade shining silver in the torchlight. "I'm not anyone."

The guard nodded and stepped aside. Finn led the Mapwalkers into the stone chamber. Sculptures of the god surrounded an altar where a number of objects lay on a white cloth. A ceremonial fire burned in front of the altar and Perry walked to it, putting his hand in the flames. He turned his hand as if coaxing the fire into his palm. His eyes reflected the fire, and it was as if his skin became burnished copper.

Mila walked to the altar. "These objects are considered relics, because they come from Earth-side. They have the energy of our civilization and act as anchors. Those Borderlanders with the right magic cross over using these objects. Do you recognize anything?"

Sienna looked closely and for a moment, she thought her father's compass lay on the cloth in front of her. Her heart beat faster, but then, she saw it had different engravings. She picked it up to look more closely.

Finn stepped close to her. "You can't touch it. Put it down." His voice was low and urgent. "The guards are watching, and we can't have them tell my father you were here. It jeopardizes my position."

Mila looked up at him. "It's a Mapwalker compass. You know we can't leave it here. We're taking it with us."

Finn's face turned to thunder. "You said you just wanted to look."

"I did, but it belonged to one of the group we're looking for." Mila shook her head. "It's time, Finn. You have to decide which side you're on."

The drums and chanting stopped. A single wail rose above the quiet, the piercing cry of a mother losing her child. The crowd roared as they celebrated the sacrifice. Sienna imagined the blood of the child shed for the hungry god, knowing it would never be enough.

The sound of running feet suddenly came from outside, then shouts as more guards arrived. Mila looked at the door and then over at Finn. "Time to make your choice."

Finn hesitated for a moment, then drew his sword.

Xander took the folded map from his pocket, laid it on the floor. The lion, Asada, stepped from the page. He roared, charging forward as guards ran into the room, swords held high, some with crossbows at the ready, arrows nocked.

Perry pulled his hand from the flame and threw a ball of fire at the guards. It exploded in the air above their heads, raining down shards of soot. The guards turned in pain, some of them on fire, running for the doorway. The lion leapt in with huge hooked paws, slicing at the guards nearest him.

"We can't hold them for long," Mila shouted. "We need to get out of here."

Sienna put the compass securely inside her jacket pocket, and they began to back away towards the far archway as Finn fought with the remaining guards.

A booming voice echoed out across the temple. "You dare to cross the god of the Tophet, my son? You would let these Earth-bastards take my relics like they have stolen our land?"

Finn turned towards his father's voice, momentarily distracted. One of the guards swooped in and slashed at him with a sword, drawing blood. Finn spun and with one sweep finished off the guard with a slice across his neck. He held his arm, blood running between his fingers, as the warlord spoke.

"You're a traitor. If you stay, I'll forgive you. But if you go with them, I will hunt you all down and your skulls will ring the pit along with the other firstborn."

Finn's face was set in a grim glare, his features carved from ebony. He took a deep breath, then turned and strode towards the Mapwalker team.

Perry summoned new life into the fire, creating a wall of flame between them and their pursuers.

"Asada, come." Xander put the map down and the lion leapt into it. Xander folded the scrap and put it back in his pocket.

Finn took the lead, running down the corridor as he shouted back at the team. "We need to get back to the souk. We'll lose them in the labyrinth. I have friends in the Resistance who will get us out the city, but we have a long way to go tonight."

They ran through narrow streets, surrounded on both sides by ruined buildings. Sounds of pursuit soon faded behind them. Finn ducked through the warren of tiny streets, turning left and right until Sienna wasn't sure which way they were going anymore, only that they had to trust this man who had turned against his father for them.

The compass seemed to pulse in her pocket. It occurred to her that she could put her hand on it and transport the Mapwalkers somewhere else. But then she looked at Finn running ahead. He had risked his life for them, walked away from his father and his life. She took her hand away from the compass.

Finn ducked into one of the many derelict houses, led them out the back and then down an underground passage. The walls dripped with water and smelled of rot and mold, the air chill. After walking for what seemed like too long in the cold darkness, they finally emerged into an ancient cistern. Two men and a woman greeted them, faces wrapped in scarves to cover their features, voices low as they talked in a language Sienna didn't recognize.

Finn turned back to the Mapwalkers. "We can stay here for now, lie low and eat. We'll continue the journey after some rest."

The woman brought them sleeping mats and a bowl of soup each. Mila took crackers from within her ration pack, handed them out, and they shared a meal together by the fire.

Perry gazed into the flames, the reflection turning his eyes a golden hue. Sienna wondered what he saw there. Could he find a way out through the fire?

Mila came and sat next to Sienna. "You still have the compass, right?"

"Of course." She looked over the fire at Finn. He was whittling a tiny horse from acacia wood, his movements graceful and precise. "What did you promise Finn in exchange for his help?"

Before Mila could speak, Finn looked over. "My sister was taken for the Halbrasse. My father exchanged her for power in this city. She's in the castle of the Shadow Cartographers." He narrowed his eyes at Mila. "And you will take me there as promised."

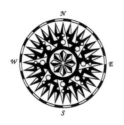

CHAPTER 13

Perry lay by the fire, looking into the flames. Sienna and Mila talked with the Borderlander, Finn, on the other side. Xander sat in the corner of the cistern, sketching in his notebook, absorbed in his drawing, like he seemed to do more and more these days. Perry cupped his hand and summoned a tiny flame in the center of his palm. He smiled. It seemed he was learning how to manage his magic at last. He thought back to the room in the citadel they had fled from. There was a moment when the fire had done his bidding. After so long struggling with control, he might finally be reaching a point where he knew how to use it.

But there was a darker current below his satisfaction.

When the flame kindled, he had felt a tug towards destruction. The difficulty in being a Fire Cartographer was walking the line between destruction and creation, between warming people and cooking food or burning everything to ash.

The marks of fire were everywhere in the Borderlands. People's homes burned down by regimes that didn't want them, the scars of burned cities on their skin. Perry wanted to be horrified, but as he had thrown the fire at those guards, their screams gave him a dark satisfaction. It disturbed him, because it was the edge of Shadow Cartography.

He remembered when he would sit with his father in the woods behind the Mercator estate gazing into the flames together. His father would light the fire with a flick of his fingers and make the flames dance as he told stories of his adventures in the Borderlands. Truth be told, his father loved the Borderlands more than he loved Earth-side and Perry was born because of his love for a Borderlander.

He was a Halbrasse.

Perry's eyes slid over to Finn, knowing the man's sister had been forced into creating half-breeds to feed the power of the Shadow Cartographers. But his own mother had not been forced into it.

Sir Douglas had met Morwenna on a mission when a Mapwalker team had come over looking for a certain artifact. His mother had been one of those guarding it, and the two had fallen in love. When the rest of the team had returned Earth-side, Sir Douglas had stayed, determined to live in the Borderlands, but the Illuminated Cartographer summoned him back. The way his father told it, the pair had been star-crossed lovers on either side of the border. Perry had been born in the Borderlands, but as he grew up, he discovered he could walk into Earth-side. Sir Douglas took him to live on the Mercator estate with all its luxury. A world away from his mother's camp.

Ten years ago, Morwenna had been killed, and one of the Mapwalkers from the Ministry was involved. His father had become distant, his trips into the Borderlands increasingly outside the rules of the Ministry.

Now Perry wrestled with where his allegiance should lie. He had friends on Earth-side, he went to school there and now he was a Mapwalker with the Ministry. He had a purpose and Perry was proud of that. And yet when he was over here, he saw the people in the Borderlands were no different. They loved, they wanted to provide for their children, they would fight for their families. And perhaps they needed more help than those who took life for granted on Earth-side.

Perry lay back and closed his eyes as his father's words echoed in memory. *The border is a construct, keeping two halves of a whole apart. Two halves which are one in you, my son.*

When the fire expanded under his skin, Perry thought he would rather live here in the Borderlands. On Earth-side, he couldn't even use the magic outside the Ministry. And what was he if not a Fire Cartographer? If he couldn't use his magic, what was the point?

* * *

After a few hours' sleep, Finn woke them up. Sienna jumped in the semi-darkness as his face loomed close to hers.

"It's okay. It's only me." He grinned. "I don't bite."

They packed up the bags and left the Resistance fighters in the cistern. They headed into the tunnels beyond and soon emerged into the far desert as dawn painted the horizon in shades of coral pink.

Sienna glanced over at Finn. He was only a few years older than she was, which meant his sister was a lot younger. No wonder he wanted to rescue her from the castle.

They walked through the desert, past scrub brushes and the ruins of old cities poking out through the sand, pieces of sculpture from lost civilizations. In the distance, a group of low mountains rose out of the sand where dunes had piled up over time. The mounds formed shapes of strange creatures as the sun rose higher. As they drew closer, a collection of small sandy dwellings could be seen nestled in the lee of the slope. They looked abandoned, used only by travelers to shelter from the scorching sun.

The detritus of those passing through littered the shack

inside. Old food tins and a tattered book, pages falling out from overuse. It was dusty and smelled like something had died and rotted there.

Finn walked to the back where a small second chamber led off the first, carved deeper into the sandstone. He beckoned, and they followed him in. He bent down and started to scrape away the sand. "I could use some help here."

Sienna and Perry got down next to him and began to sweep the dust and dirt away, revealing a trapdoor beneath. It seemed incongruous here in the middle of the desert as the trapdoor could only lead down to the sand below. Finn looked up, a smile on his face. "You won't believe what's down here."

He pulled it up. The hinges made no sound, clearly kept oiled and ready for use. The ruins and detritus were all for show.

"There are oil lamps once we get further in," Finn explained as he stepped down into the dark.

Sienna opened her mouth, ready to suggest they should just use a torch. Mila put her hand out and shook her head. "They don't have electricity here, so no batteries either. We have them just in case but we save them for emergencies."

The bright flare of a match came from down below and then the soft, warm light of an oil lamp. Sienna looked down into the trapdoor as Finn appeared at the bottom. He looked up, a lamp in his hand. "Come on down."

Sienna climbed down using stone handholds, each foot feeling for the next rung until she emerged into the passage below. She turned around, her fingers tracing chisel marks on the stone walls. The passage was narrow but tall enough so Finn could walk upright. He led them on into the dark.

"These caves were used a thousand years ago to escape the invasion of the Muslim Arabs. You know them on Earthside as part of the Derinkuyu caves. They could fit twenty thousand people down here, so the whole city could shelter in times of trouble. There were stables and cellars as well as chapels and meeting rooms." Finn smiled. "Even wine and oil presses. The important stuff."

"How were they built?" Sienna asked.

"It's soft volcanic rock, part of Cappadocia in Earth-side Turkey," Mila explained. "Pushed over the border when the caves were shut off to the public. I've heard you can cross directly here if you go through Turkey's Ministry."

Sienna found it hard to keep track of how the Borderlands related to Earth-side. Like the vellum map back in Hereford, it was as if the world had been scrunched up so the different parts touched at different points. The Borderlands were the negative space off the edges of Earth-side, constantly shifting as the world changed.

They walked on down narrow tunnels, passing places where the rooms opened out, held up by thick rock pillars. The cave walls were carved into functional shapes, places for animals to eat, alcoves to hold tiny statues of gods. The ceilings were low in some parts and Sienna couldn't help thinking of the weight of all that rock above them. But this place had stood for nearly a thousand years, so why would it fall now?

She just couldn't stop the thoughts from filling her mind. Some of the rooms were so tiny that they seemed like cells, but Sienna could see how the families felt safe down here while the world raged above. There were words carved into the rock, ancient graffiti from people who had lived and died here. She ran her fingers over the indentations, wondering about their lives.

"They had huge rocks to roll over the entrances, closing the city from inside," Finn explained. "Each separate level could be shut off. Like a castle in reverse."

"How deep is it?" Sienna asked.

"There are ten levels going all the way down to an underground river flowing beneath."

Mila turned at his words. "We need to go down there. The last team had a water walker like me, so perhaps they went that way."

They descended further, winding through the tunnels, air cooling as they went deeper. Sienna touched the water on the walls of the caves as they passed, trailing her fingers in the moisture.

They emerged into a chamber where four skeletons lay in what looked like a ritual pattern. Their heads all pointed to the center and one was propped up in the middle, one bony hand raised towards the roof.

"The five-pointed compass," Mila whispered. "It looks like Mapwalkers traveled here a long time ago. Perhaps these people sought to harness the magic somehow."

They walked into the next room.

Suddenly there was a sliding and slipping, the sound of sand washing through a chute.

"Watch out!" Finn stepped back, pushing Sienna behind him. Cracks in the ceiling opened up, dumping a huge load of rocks and sand in their path.

"I've heard there are traps down here," Finn said. "Ways to kill invaders. Things to keep people away."

They stood for a moment, listening, waiting, then walked carefully around the edge of the room and into another chamber. Fossils lined the walls, creatures that had once lived, trilobites and dinosaurs, their bones fossilized into the rock. This was a shrine to the long dead, but they stood like sentinels guarding the way.

Huge birds with sharp beaks and teeth like sharks stood either side of the doorway, their wing bones held high as if to stop anyone passing, their legs flexed ready to leap. A phalanx of fossilized sea spiders with huge articulated legs looked as if they could step out from the rock at any moment. Giant scorpions, triple the size Sienna had seen in the desert, their thick bodies full of venom, stood with arched tails ready to strike.

Around the fearsome fossils, there was a beautiful frieze of ammonites and sea creatures frozen into the rock, their colors still vibrant after so many years.

"These are amazing." Xander stepped closer and pulled out his sketchbook and pencil.

A crack of stone and crunch of rock split the air, a wrenching sound from the earth. A rumble shook the floor, sand and dust raining down on them from above. Two giant birds stepped out from the wall, articulated stone joints cracking as their empty eyes turned to look at their prey. Scorpions flicked themselves off the wall with their tails, scuttling to surround the group as spiders arched from the walls.

The creatures began to advance.

CHAPTER 14

ONE OF THE BIRDS darted in, teeth clacking together as it lunged at Finn. He spun away, pulling his sword and swinging it, taking the head of the bird off. It fell to the floor, but the bird kept coming, like a stone zombie intent on its prey.

One of the scorpions scuttled up Sienna's leg.

"How are you meant to kill a fossil?" Mila said, as she tugged the creature off, threw it to the ground and smashed it with a rock into tiny pieces until the scorpion stopped moving. Sienna picked up her own rock, and they stood back to back, fighting off the creatures together.

Xander took out his map and laid it on the ground. Nothing happened. Asada remained just an illustration on the page. Xander looked confused. "There's something different about this rock. I can't tap into earth magic."

"It's volcanic, made of lava," Finn shouted as he smashed the pommel of his sword down onto a spider, crushing its body to the floor.

Perry put his hand on the rock, trying to sense something that would help them. The birds advanced, bones clicking. The scorpions and spiders stalked across the floor towards them. He didn't have much time.

This rock had been made from fire, so maybe he could unmake it. He put his hand flat on the wall and concentrated on making the rock molten again. It softened and began to burn.

He pulled a ball of molten rock from the wall and threw it at one of the fossil birds. The fiery ball smashed through its head, and its bones began to melt in the flames. The others ducked away from the ash, falling back behind him.

Perry stepped forward and put his hands to the ground. Jets of flame came out of his hands, zoomed across the floor and soon the stone creatures were melting, becoming one with the volcanic rock again.

As the creatures melted into the floor, Perry watched the flames dance closer to his team. The Borderlander rose inside him and for a moment, he wanted to keep it burning.

He shook his head, lifting his hands from the floor as if they suddenly burned. These thoughts came every time he used his Mapwalker power. He had to be careful.

"We need to get going," Perry said. "I can sense there are more of these creatures down here. I can't melt them all."

They continued through the narrow stone passageway, down into the depths of the cave system. The dripping of water intensified and soon they could hear the quiet rush of a stream.

They emerged at the bottom of the cave system into a final chamber carved with images of a goddess. Tiamat of ancient Babylon, goddess of chaos and primordial creation, a sea serpent with curled tail wrapped around a sacrifice.

"The storm god Moloch killed her and the heavens and the earth formed from her slaughtered body." Mila ran her hand over the stone coils. "She's a powerful water goddess, ruling where the salt meets fresh." Mila turned to look into the dark waters flooding part of the chamber and led into the underground waterway. "There must be a reason she's worshipped down here." She pointed. "Look towards the back of the cave."

The coils of a great serpent rose from the water and then

sunk back down again. The creature of Tiamat was still here.

Mila walked to the water's edge and put her hand into the water. "This is where the sacrifice would be made to guarantee safe passage. I guess no one is volunteering." She looked around, one eyebrow raised. "I can go into the water. There must be a boat around here somewhere, something you can travel in as I propel you past."

Finn's dark skin seemed suddenly pale. "You didn't tell me we had to cross water."

"Why are you so scared?" Sienna asked.

"The sea and the rivers bleed into Earth-side. If I cross the border …" He shook his head.

"What would happen?" Sienna asked.

"I disappear into the shadow plane, cease to exist, although no one truly knows." Finn shrugged. "Many of us dream of crossing the border and seeing your side of the world, but it's just not possible."

"What if someone were to take you safely across?" Sienna asked.

"Who would do that?" Finn said.

"Here's a boat," Xander shouted from the corner of the cave. "It's old, but it might still be okay."

It was a coracle, a small round boat made of woven reeds and covered in pitch.

"Looks safe enough," Perry said, examining it closely.

Sienna couldn't imagine going too far in the bedraggled craft, but there was no other choice. "I guess we have to try."

They carried the coracle to the water. As they approached, the coils of the giant sea serpent came closer as if sensing their vibrations.

"Are you sure about this?" Sienna looked doubtfully towards the creature.

Mila nodded. "I know water." She gazed out over the darkness. "And I know her." Mila's skin already shimmered and she looked like she wanted to sink into the black.

There wasn't much room in the coracle, and they were all crushed together, Finn's hard body up against Sienna's. As Mila pushed the boat away from the shore, Sienna found herself leaning into him, finding solace in his warmth.

Perry held one of the lamps high as Mila slipped into the water behind them, her body shimmering as she became one with the liquid, disappearing beneath. The boat began to move through the cave system. Sienna looked down to see if she could see her friend, but the water was black and there was nothing but a ripple in their wake.

The great coils of the serpent dipped below the surface of the water and then disappeared. For a moment they looked around waiting for it to emerge but all was quiet, the lapping of water on the rocky sides of the cave system the only sound.

Stalactites hung down from the ceiling, great spikes of rock formed over the years dipping down to almost touch the water. The air smelled of minerals and salt. In some places the ceiling was so low they had to duck down, huddling together as the coracle edges bumped against the rocks. Sienna felt Finn tense at these moments, and she remembered his fear of being lost between worlds. She trailed her fingers in the water and thought of happy times on the beach. The waves were pleasure and freedom to her. How different it was in the Borderlands.

Time passed slowly as they moved through the deep waters of the cave system until finally, there was a shimmer of light in the distance that grew into a shaft of daylight beyond. As they came closer, a tall arch emerged from the darkness, carved from the rock, a portal to the outside. Beyond them, in the distance, blue water stretched to the horizon. Fruit-covered branches hung down over the entrance, and as they pushed through, the air was suddenly bright and filled with birdsong.

Finn reached up and grabbed one of the fruits, plucking it from the branch. "Do you have peaches Earth-side?"

"Of course." Sienna laughed.

Finn used the edge of his sword to cut the warm peach into four and shared it amongst them. Sweetness exploded on Sienna's tongue, a taste of summer. The boat edged towards a shoreline where stones made a tiny beach on the side of an island. The coracle pushed into the shallows and then Mila emerged from the water. She shivered, her skin still shimmering.

"You alright?" Sienna asked.

Mila nodded. "I just need a minute in the sun. It's the main problem with being a warm-blooded creature in a cold-blooded world. I haven't quite got the hang of staying warm while in the water." She looked around. "I wonder where we are. I don't recognize this place."

A path led up from the beach into dense forest. Crooked trees wound around each other, and parasitic plants on the trunks sapped their strength. The interior was an impenetrable dark green.

"We have two choices," Mila said. "We go back in the water, and I see where else I can take us." She turned and pointed to the water, where blue ocean stretched to the horizon. "Or we go up onto this island and see where the hell we are."

A screech came from the forest ahead of them. The sound of flapping wings and then a shadow fell upon the beach. Sienna looked up to see a huge silhouette against the sky, the bird's outstretched wings spanning thirty feet, much wider than any bird she had seen before. Its beak was a sharp hook as big as a scythe, and she could almost feel its gaze upon them, looking down from where it circled above. She wondered whether it could see through the border and how far away they were from its porous edge. It cried again, and there was an answering call in the distance.

Xander leaned back, his hand over his eyes as he focused on the bird. "Argentavis magnificens, extinct on Earth-side," he said with a smile. "We should discuss this at the forest's edge. They're hunters and big enough to carry one of us away."

CHAPTER 15

SIENNA FELT A TUG towards the interior of the island, through the darkness of the trees and onwards. She was sure the dark castle lay ahead of them on land, not by sea anymore.

"It's this way." Her voice was confident.

"Agreed," Finn said. "And I much prefer land to water." He took a few steps towards the trees and looked up at them. Sienna walked forward to join him. The dense foliage smelled of wet earth and moss, overlaid by the mold of dead leaves. A low buzz came from the semidarkness ahead, and Sienna caught sight of clouds of flying insects within.

"Looks like fun." Finn grinned.

Sienna pulled the sleeves of her top down, covering as much skin as possible as she smiled back. She was glad Finn was there. He was an outsider and as unsure of his place in the makeshift team as she was. They were a strange group, each with their own agenda. She turned to look back at the others. Mila stood facing the water, arms wrapped around herself as if she held herself back from diving into the blue and swimming away. Perry and Xander pulled the coracle further up away from the water's edge, bantering back and forth.

Sienna didn't know their individual reasons for being part of the Mapwalker team, but she understood Finn and his desire to free his sister. As long as they headed towards the castle, Finn would stay with them. And for that, she was glad.

Finn took a step into the forest and Sienna went after him, the others close behind. Within a few meters, the beach was out of sight. The canopy of trees rose above like a prison in shades of green with bars of thick tree trunks, hung with lianas, around them. The springy ground was dense with plants and entwined roots, tendrils wrapped around her ankles and seemed to drag back every step. The air had an intense humidity, every breath a gulp. Sweat trickled down Sienna's spine, and her clothes clung to her as moisture soaked through.

It was as if the land was decomposing, the body of the earth rotting, each footstep sinking into a bog of dead flesh. The ground opened like a huge dark mouth, roots of trees like decayed teeth waiting to devour any who stepped inside. The forest canopy cast a dark shadow, vines hanging down like sinister tentacles, a path of obstacles, an entangled world where chaos reigned.

Finn strode ahead, using his sword to chop down branches in their path. He was clearly used to the swing of it, his strokes confident. Sienna found herself mesmerized by the movement of the muscles on his back, his breath even as they pushed on.

"I think I came here a long time ago with my father," he called back. "We were on a hunt for wild pigs." His voice faltered. "But something else came out of the forest. I still don't know if we really saw it, or whether I just remember something that scared me as a child. But we didn't stay long after it had passed." He turned, and his eyes met Sienna's. "I'm sure it was nothing."

Sienna thought back to the warlord who ordered child sacrifice at the Tophet. What would scare a man like that?

It started to rain as they walked on and soon the ground

was slick with mud, their feet soaked through. The sound of rain dripping on leaves was a calm meditation, a welcome respite from the crazy pace of the last day. Sienna turned her face up so the cool drops touched her skin, glimpsing the sky through the canopy of leaves above. A sky that linked such diverse environments. On Earth-side, she would have to fly, drive, then trek huge distances to get between a buried Turkish city of lava and a jungle like this. Yet here in the Borderlands, they rubbed up against each other, pushed together by the ridges in the map.

Suddenly, Sienna thought she saw something move in the trees, a shadow swinging like a monkey, jumping from branch to branch. A hoot rang out, a low sound that echoed around them.

The group stopped, bunching together back to back as they faced out into the jungle. Finn held his sword in front of him, arms wide in a fighting stance. The hoot came again, and it sent a shiver down Sienna's spine.

"Any idea what it is?"

Finn shook his head. "But we need to keep moving. We have to be out of here before it gets dark."

They walked on, ducking under huge branches and climbing over logs.

"Keep an eye out as we walk," Finn said. "Look for slimy and scaly textures that stand out against the leaves. And don't touch anything. Try not to put your hand out even to help yourself over a log. That's when you're most likely to get bitten."

Sienna wondered what kind of first-aid knowledge the team had between them, what training they had in general. She was the newbie, and in the haste of the expedition, she had missed out on whatever passed for the standard training program. But she trusted Finn to keep them safe. He took the lead here, this was his land, after all.

She felt a sharp sting on her arm and slapped at a

mosquito the size of a coin. A splash of blood exploded from its body onto her skin. Sienna grimaced. It would be crazy to die of a mosquito bite in a jungle only miles from downtown Bath. She shook her head in wonder.

"Oh, that is cool." Xander's voice rang out.

Sienna turned to see him gazing at something on the trunk of a palm tree. A huge spider with a body as big as her hand and legs as long as her arm. It squatted on the bark, seemingly oblivious to their presence.

Xander pulled out his sketchbook and began to draw, sure strokes quickly recreating the shape of the spider on his page. He bent closer, and the spider reared up, fangs dripping venom. As Xander backed away, his eyes fixed on the creature, a smile on his face, Sienna couldn't help wondering what he did with his drawings. If he could only illustrate on maps created by others, did he have some pile of discarded maps with monsters on them ready to emerge into the world?

The rain grew heavier. The smell of the jungle intensified with the must of mold and the heavy fragrance of tropical flowers. Sienna felt suddenly alive. She had been slowly dying in the never-ending grind of her job back in Oxford. But this was adventure. This was geography made life.

She looked around with new eyes, noting the jungle seemed more Latin American than African. It was certainly as wet as the Amazon. A place where everything fought to survive, from the bugs biting through her shirt to the parasitic plants wound around the trees, up the food chain to the apex predators.

She tried not to think what they might be.

A skittering noise came from a log next to them. A giant centipede scurried across, its segmented body over a meter long in shades of ochre and orange. The striped legs all moved separately, and its head waved around as its antennae scanned ahead.

"This place is awesome," Xander said, with a wide grin.

A sharp cry rang out. They turned to see Perry wrapped in the coils of a huge snake, its muscled body completely encasing him.

"Titanoboa." Finn leapt forward, his sword outstretched to cut Perry free.

"Wait, don't harm it." Xander stepped in front. "It's a constrictor, so Perry has a moment. Let me try."

Xander reached out to touch the skin of the boa. Sienna recalled that such a creature, the largest snake ever discovered, had become extinct millions of years ago on Earthside. But these huge ancient creatures clearly thrived in the Borderlands.

Perry gasped as the coils tightened, his eyes wide with panic.

Xander stepped closer to the snake, its scales shining as rain dripped off them, rainbow colors on a copper skin marked with bands of black. The snake's head stretched out towards him, its tongue flickering. He stood there, letting the snake taste his skin, eyes closed as if he was communing with it. Sienna glimpsed the predator in him, a reflection of the reptile, perhaps.

Finn stepped closer, his sword raised. "Hurry."

Then, as suddenly as it had arrived, the boa unwrapped its coils from Perry's body. He dropped to the ground and the snake curled around the branch above.

Xander ran his hand along the boa's length, whispering something to it. When he turned, his eyes were as black as the snake's. Sienna blinked, and his eyes were green again.

"Time to go," he said. "It will be dark soon."

Mila put her arm around Perry's waist, supporting him until he caught his breath. They walked on through the jungle, stumbling over hidden branches as the light faded. It seemed like it would never end but then at last, there was a break in the trees ahead.

The quality of light changed from tropical green to a dull, cold grey as they approached. The edge of the jungle was a bright line where verdant foliage ended, and as they stepped out of the rainforest, Sienna could see derelict buildings clustered ahead of them, overgrown with weeds. The smell changed from lush jungle to the scent of smoke.

Tendrils of the forest reached out as if life wanted to encroach here but the green shoots curled up, dying on the black, brackish soil. The change in the landscape was disconcerting, like jumping through time and space all at once.

Finn bent and picked up handful of the soil, bringing it to his nose to smell. He rubbed it between his fingers before dropping it back to the ground, then wiped his hands on his clothes.

"I think this is Poveglia. I've heard rumors of it. They say the soil here is fifty percent human, made from burned and buried bodies." He frowned, looking ahead to the ruins. "They say it's cursed."

CHAPTER 16

Finn looked back into the forest. It was almost dark. He gestured ahead. "Whatever is here, it has to be safer than the jungle at night. Let's find a place to sleep."

They walked on, catching sight of a towering spire ahead, jutting out from the low buildings and stunted trees, and covered with twisted foliage. The sky was the shade of bruised plums, a sickening purple and black that barely lit the way ahead. The rain was gentler, but the ground was muddy underfoot and the wind a biting chill, as they walked on towards what had to be their haven for the night.

Finn dropped back to walk beside Sienna. "They say this was once an institution for the mentally ill and a quarantine island for those with the plague Earth-side. There are even rumors of experiments done on those the world wanted to forget."

They passed huge ovens with crumbling brick walls and metal doors hanging off rusty hinges. Sienna nodded towards them. "I suppose they needed to bake a lot of bread to feed all those people."

Finn shook his head with a half-smile. "Those are not for baking bread. The guards would shovel the dead into pits here, and when they were full, they would burn the bodies. Many of them weren't even dead, merely a step away from the end. My father thought about using this place as some kind of outpost." He looked up at the bell tower ahead of them. "But no one would stay here."

The path wound towards the bell tower around the edge of a deep pit. Sienna walked closer.

Finn put a hand on her arm. "Don't."

But she couldn't resist her curiosity. She walked closer and stared over the edge. Skeletons lay tangled together, their skulls facing in alternate directions on top of a jumble of long femurs, spines and pelvic bones.

There were so many.

The pit stretched as far as she could see in both directions. She raised a hand to her mouth, swallowing down the bile that rose. But she couldn't look away. Who were these people? Had they been pushed over into the Borderlands during life or only after death?

As she gazed at the bones, she could see they had been lying here for a very long time. There was no flesh left on them, and the pit smelled only of earth. Sienna frowned and bent closer as she noticed one of the skulls had a brick shoved between its teeth. What the –?

Finn came and stood by her side, noticing what she looked at. "It's a shroud eater," he said. "Some thought them to be vampires that fed on the bloody cloth surrounding the dead and then spread the plague to bring more victims. The brick forced into the vampire's mouth supposedly stopped it feeding and starved it to death." He shrugged. "Or maybe that's why they started burning people. To get rid of the food supply."

"It's horrible." Sienna pointed into the pit. "There are children in there."

Finn sighed. "There are places here in the Borderlands your people on Earth-side chose to forget. But you can't write people out of history, no matter what you do. There *are* witnesses, but they lie dead over here."

Sienna saw a hunger for justice on his face and a search for some kind of truth in this brutal place. Perhaps not all witnesses were in the grave.

Finn turned, and they walked on towards shelter. As they approached, details emerged from the semi-darkness. The bell tower had cracks through the stone, gaping holes and glassless windows, exposed bricks and broken walls, lichen crawling up its side. The crumbled state of the buildings reflected the fallen state of the world. This place had once been alive and beautiful, and now it was decayed and forgotten.

At the bell tower, they pushed open an old door hanging off its hinges. Inside at least there were walls and a roof, shelter from the cold wind and the rain.

They walked through an entrance hall with bars on the windows to keep those inside from escaping. The place was a strange juxtaposition of medieval plague pit and modern psychiatric hell. Vines grew through every window, and ceilings had collapsed in most of the rooms, rotted beams dropping down with the pervasive smell of mold and rot. The empty ruins had only a faint echo of the life that had once walked here.

They passed one room where jagged holes and lumps of metal riddled the walls, the edges still sharp.

"What happened here?" Sienna asked.

"A group of prisoners got hold of a hand grenade," Finn said. "They gathered tightly around it and pulled the pin. Their bodies were blown apart and the shrapnel embedded in the walls around us. That's one way out of hell, I suppose."

They walked on and found a room with a row of bed frames stacked against peeling wallpaper. The window was intact, there was no draught, and it felt warmer than the rest of the building. There was even a fireplace with decorative blue and white tiles covered in dust and ash. Underneath, birds flew over an expanse of ocean.

"Home, sweet home." Perry crossed to the fireplace. He grabbed a piece of discarded metal from a bed frame and poked around up the chimney. "Looks alright. I'll get the fire going. Then at least we can warm ourselves."

There was plenty of wooden furniture in the rooms around them. They collected rickety old chairs, breaking them against the walls to make smaller pieces. Perry conjured a flame, and soon they were warm and drying themselves in front of the fire. Perry got out his travel kettle and began boiling water. "Anyone else for tea?"

Sienna sipped the hot drink, considering how much better everything seemed to be inside a shelter with warmth. Perhaps things weren't so bad, after all.

As the others huddled around the fire, she suddenly had an acute desire to get away, craving some solitude after what had been a confusing and crazy twenty-four hours. Had it only been yesterday when she had heard of her grandfather's death?

She stood up. "I'm going to take a look around."

"I'll come with you," Mila said, standing up and dusting off her cargo pants.

"If you don't mind, I'd just like some space."

Mila paused and then nodded. "Of course, but don't go too far. Holler if you need us."

Sienna stepped outside the room and walked a little way in the semi-darkness, listening to the voices of the team fading behind her. She pulled her pack open and found the torch. Mila said it was only for emergencies, but she wouldn't be long.

She walked down the corridor, her footsteps an echo of the past, clouds of dust rising in her wake. She shone the torch into the rooms on either side, catching glimpses of broken furniture, desks and chairs, and then in one, the light glinted off a metal cage.

Sienna stepped into the room, playing the light over the

structure. As she walked closer, she saw a skeleton curled at the bottom, its arms wrapped around its head, a defensive posture it must have died in. She had read enough about the history of psychiatry to know about the atrocities committed in the name of science, but the cage was still disturbing.

A scratching sound came from the corner and Sienna spun around, her torchlight catching the thick tail of something furry as it scurried into a hole in the wall. A rat. Much bigger than anything she'd seen before. She shuddered to think of the food supply that would have sustained creatures here.

There was a door near the cage, and she opened it to find a small padded room beyond, the cushioned walls covered in lichen and mold. Rain dripped through a hole in the ceiling. Although the space was clearly man-made, it felt like nature was reclaiming this asylum, one room at a time. She shut the door and went back out to the corridor.

She turned to see the rosy glow of the fire coming from a doorway far back up where she had walked from. She considered returning to the team, but she was relishing this time alone. Sienna walked on and found a huge ballroom with a wooden floor that must have once been polished to a shine. Painted panels of flowers and fruit covered the walls. A pile of old suitcases in faded primary colors lay covered in dust and broken masonry from the partially caved-in ceiling.

A piano stood against one wall. She touched a key, and a dull note echoed in the room. A skittering noise came from within the instrument. She backed away and turned towards the end of the ballroom where another door led away from the main corridor. Sienna walked on into the heart of the institution.

In the middle of the next room, a dentist's chair sat, fully reclinable, but with thick leather straps for the wrists, ankles and head. A sink in the corner overflowed with ferns and moss, verdant life in the ruins. Next to it, a metal table with drawers covered in thick cobwebs. Sienna used her sleeve to brush them away and pulled the drawer open. A syringe with a thick needle lay next to a series of scalpels, the blades glinting in the light. The edges still looked sharp enough. She picked one up and wrapped the end in a piece of rag, slipping it into her pack before walking on. It made her feel better to have a makeshift weapon.

The next room had once been a morgue, the thick doors open wide to display racks of shelving behind. There were nine slots tapering into darkness and Sienna couldn't help thinking of who might have lain here last. They must have been important to avoid the grave pits outside.

Around the walls, there were racks of shelving with glass jars and test-tubes arrayed upon them. The jars were covered in dust, but there were shadows inside. Sienna reached up and brushed the front of one then recoiled as the side of a diseased face turned towards her in the liquid.

A rustling sound came from behind her.

She turned as a rat burst out from the shadows, running across the floor towards her. Sienna jumped, a gasp escaping her throat. The rat was big as a dog, its teeth bared as it approached, red eyes fixed on her.

Then out of the shadows, more emerged.

They moved as a pack, black-bristled fur over muscled bodies and thick pink tails like rope. The biggest rat darted in, teeth snapping. Sienna backed away and climbed quickly onto a gurney against the wall, pulling her feet out of its way just in time.

The pack ran forward, furry bodies clustering around the gurney, moving it on squeaky wheels as they swirled around the metal legs. A stench of feces and rotting flesh rose up from the pack and Sienna gagged as she looked down into the vortex of bodies. They looked up at her with the fixation of hungry animals desperate for a meal.

"Help!" she cried. "Finn! Mila? Anyone?"

She thumped on the gurney sending a metallic ringing sound out into the corridor. But there was no sound of running feet, no voices. She had wandered too far.

She was alone.

Sienna thought back to how she had sat in the stacks of the Bodleian, lost in the books, not knowing which way to go. Back then, she had to use someone else's map to escape, but Mila had said *anything* could be a map for a Blood Cartographer. She could create her own map and walk through it.

She looked down at the stinking rats with their sharp yellow teeth.

It was worth a try.

Sienna pulled the scalpel from her pack and looked at the blade, then down at the rats. She could use it as a weapon and try to get out of here. She could wait for someone to rescue her, or she could see what she was capable of.

She winced in anticipation of the pain. "It won't hurt, it won't hurt," she whispered, then sliced into her forearm.

It did hurt, and she didn't even want to consider the diseases she might have given herself with the dirty blade. But it was better than getting eaten by giant rats.

As blood welled up, she used the fingertips of her other hand to dab a little of the liquid and then started to paint on the wall. She visualized the asylum and the corridors she had walked through, sketching the lines of the area where the team waited.

She drew the dimensions of the room and the pathway to the outside where skeletons lay in their eternal rest. She sensed the orientation of the building on the earth beneath and drew her compass rose beside the sketch, with its true north an echo of what she felt inside. It was like a magnet pulling her closer and Sienna gasped as she glimpsed the intoxicating power of her blood.

But would it be enough? What if she couldn't make it work?

The rats snarled below, bumping against the gurney. As she rocked from side to side, she closed her eyes and placed her hand in the middle of the rough, bloody map.

CHAPTER 17

SIENNA'S FINGERS TINGLED AS she thought of Perry and his kettle of tea, Finn whittling his running horse, Xander sketching and Mila staring into the flames. She brought life to the map in her mind and felt a lifting inside, the world as three-dimensional space below her.

Then she was back, sucked into the room where the fire burned and the team sat waiting. Sienna opened her eyes to see them all staring at her.

"Holy crap, you gave me a fright," Mila said. "Thought you were a ghost or something." She grinned. "Guess you're getting better at Mapwalking then."

Sienna nodded. "I ... I got a bit lost." Her voice shook as the intensity of the experience rocked through her. Her breath came fast, and she sat down heavily by the fire.

Perry held out a mug of tea. "You look like you had a scare. This will help."

Sienna took it and sipped for a moment. She felt their eyes upon her.

"There were giant rats," Sienna said when she got her breath back.

Finn jumped up. "Mutant cloud rats." He began to pull the bed frames in front of the door. "Quickly, help me." Perry and Mila stacked the gaps with broken furniture as

Finn explained. "Supposedly, they escaped from some experimental lab on Earth-side, and they've found plenty to eat in the Borderlands. There are stories of them ravaging villages, swarming and devouring anything in their path. There can't be too many of them here though as there's not enough food to support a colony."

"There were enough of them," Sienna said.

Finn turned and met her eyes, nodding at her unspoken horror. "We'll watch in pairs while the others get some sleep. It's a few hours until dawn, and then we can be on our way when the rats sleep."

Xander yawned. "Wake me when it's my shift." He pulled his sleeping bag around himself and rolled over with his back to the fire.

Mila put a hand on Sienna's shoulder. "Get some rest. I'll take first watch with Finn."

* * *

Bristled bodies pinned her down and sharp teeth ripped at her flesh as she screamed for help. Sienna sat up sharply, gasping for breath.

"It's okay." Perry put a hand on her arm. "Must be a nightmare. You're safe."

His voice was calming, and he reached for the kettle, pouring her a steaming cup of tea. "Here you go."

"Is tea your answer to everything?" Sienna took a sip.

Perry gave a wry smile. "I have more questions than answers, to be honest, but I find tea helps me live with them."

Dawn filtered through the barred windows, casting a sickly pale light over the team. Mila lay curled next to the fire, sleeping bag pulled up over her head. Finn lay resting on his back, hand on his sword. His eyes were open, and he looked ready to spring into action. Xander sat on the pile of broken furniture, sketching.

"You should have woken me," Sienna said. "I would have taken my turn."

Perry shook his head. "Oh, don't worry. You're new, and Mapwalking takes it out of you. Surely Bridget told you about it?"

"She didn't tell me much really. It all happened so fast. What do you mean?"

Xander stopped sketching and looked over at her, his eyes wide. "You don't know?"

Mila turned inside her sleeping bag and sat up, rubbing her eyes. "I should have told you, but I thought we'd have more time before you used it properly." She took a deep breath. "Mapwalking comes with a cost. Every time you use it in the Borderlands, you exchange your blood for a drop of shadow and you begin to change. If you use it too much, you can't cross back into Earth-side."

Perry stirred the embers of the fire, his face troubled. "That's how Shadow Cartographers are born."

Mila continued. "And it's why Bridget can't come through anymore, or some of the older Mapwalkers. They can't risk it."

Her words echoed through Sienna's mind, and she imagined the taint of darkness seeping through her veins. Her skin prickled at the thought, and the cut throbbed on her arm. "How many times can I use it safely?"

"There's no way of knowing." Xander's hazel eyes fixed on hers. "Every Mapwalker is different, and the amount of blood needed depends on the journey ... and the number of people you carry with you."

"It's why we can't just use our magic all the time," Mila said. "And why we let you rest. We need you for the next part of the journey." She took a deep breath, looking at Sienna with an apology in her eyes. "You might as well know this too. The most powerful maps are all made from the skin of Blood Cartographers. They are most effective if they are used without a drop of shadow in them. Those are the master maps, the ones protecting the border."

"The younger the skin, the less traveled, the better the map," Xander said. "Your flesh and blood are the most precious thing we have."

"That's why the Shadow Cartographers are breeding Halbrasse." Finn sat up, his face contorted with anger. "They skin the children and use rare blood to make new maps."

"It's true." Mila nodded. "And we can't keep up on Earthside because we don't countenance breeding programs. They will soon outnumber us."

Finn looked at Sienna. "You have to leave the Borderlands. If they take you, they will –"

"I'm here for my father." She thought of him held captive, bled for the ink that the Shadow Cartographers would tattoo on the skins of half-breed children. Nausea churned her stomach. She stood up. "We need to go. It's light outside and time to move on."

"Wait, I think we might be back on charted territory now, so I might be able to navigate better." Mila unrolled a skin map from her bag and pointed to the labyrinth drawn upon it. "Bridget gave me this. When it was made, the labyrinth pushed right up against Poveglia. It can't have moved too far from here."

Sienna touched the edge of the map, finally understanding the pedigree of the leather. "Whose is it?" she said, softly.

"It's old." Mila stroked the edges. "But Bridget said it was given willingly." She looked up at Sienna. "It is the fate of Blood Cartographers to become the maps that guide us."

Sienna looked down at the twisting lines of the labyrinth, and for a moment, she felt like running. She could use her magic one last time, use the star map to get back to Bath, sell the shop to Sir Douglas Mercator and move to London. Live a normal life. But would she really be able to live with the knowledge of the Borderlands out here? And could she leave her father to be bled dry in a shadowy dungeon?

Finn bent to the map and traced a line to the side of Poveglia Island. "The greater part of the jungle is new in this area, pushed through recently, but if this is accurate, I think its incursion would have pushed the labyrinth to the south-west. Here." He pointed to an area of swampland, marked on the map by reed symbols. "It's a few hours on foot."

They packed up and walked into the dawn, silent except for the tread of their feet on the hard earth. Sienna looked up as the sun broke through the clouds, turning her face to the warmth of the rays. It was strange to think the same sun shone down on Earth-side and the Borderlands alike when so much was different over here.

This land was off the edge of the maps she had studied at school, its lines inverse to the borders she knew by heart. As a child, Sienna had learned the capital cities of every country, testing herself against the map of the world on her bedroom wall. After her father had disappeared, her mother tore it down and removed every atlas from the house. But the color-coded countries were so fixed in her brain she could recall them even now.

The Borderlands were on the other side, the fifth point of the compass, and as places from Earth-side were pushed through, they ended up here crushed up against each other, pushing older places towards the Uncharted. Its very name called to something in her, a desire to go deeper into this untamed land. She was starting to understand why the Shadow Cartographers fell so far.

"What's the difference between a labyrinth and a maze?" Perry asked, breaking the silence as they walked. "I mean, what are we expecting to find?"

"Technically, a labyrinth has only one way in and one way out," Mila said. "And one way to reach the center. It's not meant to be difficult to navigate."

Perry frowned. "What's the point then?"

"Most labyrinths are ritualistic or spiritually significant,"

Sienna explained. "So the path may be winding, but there is only one route to the center, or to God. The faithful walk to the middle of the labyrinth to ritually kill Satan in a triumph over death."

"Or the monster at the heart of the labyrinth," Xander noted. "Like the Minotaur, half-bull, half-man who devoured the tribute of young men and women in ancient Crete."

Sienna remembered going with her father to visit Chartres Cathedral one summer years ago, part of a father-daughter field trip to see some of France. But now she wondered what he was really doing there since clearly, he had kept so much about his life a secret.

They had stood in front of the rose labyrinth, set into the flagstones of the nave in the Gothic cathedral. Her father explained that pilgrims had walked this labyrinth for a thousand years. The site had originally been dedicated to a fertility goddess and the Church built upon it to honor the Virgin Mary, who gave birth to a god who would save mankind. Perhaps the obsession of the Shadow Cartographers stemmed from this myth, the birth of a powerful Mapwalker who would enable them to reshape the border.

"So what about a maze?" Perry asked. "Is it just more complicated?"

"There are multiple ways in and out, dead ends and choices where you might end up trapped." Mila looked at the map again. "I think where we're going is a labyrinth, so it should be simple enough."

Finn turned at her words. "My father has sent people here before. Two commanders who betrayed him were given the choice of the fire sacrifice or the labyrinth. They chose this way, but they never returned."

They walked on in silence. The sun rose higher in the sky, and the mist burned off. Before them, a vast wall of bright green stretched across the horizon.

"More jungle?" Mila asked. "Have we come the wrong way?"

Finn shook his head. "Look at the height. It's exactly the same all the way across. It has to be a man-made barrier."

They walked on and soon they could see a giant hedge rising above them with thick, impenetrable foliage stretching as far as the eye could see in either direction. Branches and leaves intertwined in layers, so it would take an age to hack their way through. Each branch had hooked thorns, like a barbed wire fence preventing anyone from passing.

Finn looked along the hedge in both directions. "I can't see where an entrance might be. Is it marked on your map, Mila?"

As they bent over to examine it, Sienna walked up close to the hedge. There was not a leaf out of place, and the top of it was neatly trimmed. She tried to imagine whose job it might be to keep it so pristine, but then again, things worked differently over here. It smelled of the wild highlands and native herbs but underneath, an animal note of musk.

There was something, perhaps someone, alive inside.

CHAPTER 18

SIENNA RAISED HER HAND and pressed it against the hedge, feeling the prickle of branches against her palm. Suddenly, she felt a pulse of energy from within the labyrinth, something pulling her forward.

Blood answering to blood.

This had to be the right direction. She pressed her palm more firmly and felt the prick of a thorn pierce her skin. She pulled her hand away sharply to see a trickle of blood running down the center.

But where the drop of ruby liquid touched them, the branches started unraveling, twisting away from each other with a creaking and rustling sound, opening up a hole in the wall. The others turned to watch as the space grew until there was an arch big enough for them to walk through in single file.

"If in doubt, bleed on it." Xander raised an eyebrow. "Are you okay?"

She nodded, rubbing at the tiny wound in her palm.

Finn stepped through the thick tangle of branches first, his sword raised, eyes darting to either side as he scouted for danger. He nodded back to them, and the others followed him inside. The animal smell was almost overpowering.

"Careful now," he whispered. "There's something here.

Keep your voices low." He looked at Sienna. "Which way?"

She glanced in either direction. Both ways were exactly the same, long corridors of green with towering hedges boxing both sides. How was she supposed to decide?

Her palm throbbed. Mila's words echoed back to her, about how each use of blood magic let a little shadow inside to take its place. But the minutes ticked by and she couldn't think of any other way, so she placed her palm against the hedge directly in front of the entrance they had made. Perhaps the maze itself would lead the way.

Once again, the branches untwisted, opening a space into the next corridor. But this time, the sound of breaking branches and a soft huffing noise came from beyond.

Xander poked his head around the corner before anyone could stop him and then ducked back quickly, his eyes bright with excitement. "Gigantopithecus," he whispered. "A giant ape. Extinct on Earth-side but this one looks like drawings I've seen."

Sienna walked into the gap in the hedge and peered around the side, Finn close behind her.

A giant ape stood on its hind legs picking off foliage from the top of the hedge, displaying its full height of over ten feet. Its meaty hands were the size of giant baseball mitts and its thigh muscles the width of tree trunks. It grabbed a handful of leaves and put them in its mouth, chewing as it dropped back onto its knuckles. Then it looked in their direction. Sienna felt a jolt of adrenalin as it met her eyes.

"Look down," Finn breathed. "Back away slowly."

They edged their way back into the branches as the ape lumbered along the corridor towards them, the thump of its great fists shaking the earth. Sienna's mind raced as she considered how in hell she was meant to shut the opening she had made. Her blood opened a path, but she couldn't take it back.

"Don't run or it will charge," Xander said quickly. "If it's like other apes, it won't attack if we're submissive. Bow your heads as it comes through. Don't meet its eyes."

The giant ape pushed through the branches. They cracked and ripped apart across its huge barrel chest as it emerged and stood tall. It slapped its chest and bared its teeth, roaring a challenge. Sienna kept her eyes down, her heart pounding as the vibrations of its call rippled through her. She saw Finn's hand tighten on its sword and willed him not to use it. Perhaps the ape would lose interest and move off.

But it took a huge step forward towards them and swung its giant fist.

Mila dove sideways, rolling away as the meaty arm slammed down where she had stood just a moment before.

"Guess submission doesn't work." Xander pulled the skin map from his pocket, dropped it to the ground as he bellowed, drawing the beast's attention away as Asada, his lion, stepped from the leather.

The lion roared and charged at the ape, barreling into its great body, knocking the beast to the ground. But the ape put its great arms around the lion and shoved it away enough to swing a giant fist into Asada's face. The lion rolled away, snarling, the roars of the two beasts combining into a fearsome cacophony.

They ran at each other, the ape howling as the lion attacked. Dust exploded into the air as the two gigantic creatures tussled, the lion slicing and biting, the ape thumping and rolling.

A slash of claws, and bright blood flew from the ape's chest.

It turned and bit deep into the lion's flank, and the big cat yelped with pain. They were well matched, but then the wound in the lion's side healed over, and its ferocity redoubled. It slashed and bit and tore at the ape, beating it down, tiring it until the great creature lay on the ground, chest heaving, its blood soaking the earth.

The lion bent its muzzle to the wound in the ape's chest and began to tear strips of flesh from it. The ape moaned in pain as it was eaten alive, the sound so similar to a human in distress that tears sprang to Sienna's eyes. The ape was some kind of distant ancestor, despite how wild this one was. Xander watched with a dark satisfaction on his face, almost as if he was the one feeding.

Then a throaty roar came from behind the maze wall in front of them.

The lion looked up, muzzle coated with blood. It stood motionless, and Finn drew his sword again. Another roar answered – and another. There were more giant apes, and they heard one of their own in pain.

They were coming.

"Run." Xander pushed Sienna ahead of him. "Get the path opened in front of us."

He dropped back, calling Asada to stand with him, Finn on his other side, sword drawn, Mila next to him.

"Come on." Perry dragged Sienna away. "We've got to find a way through. The others will follow."

They turned a corner, and Sienna felt a tug inwards. "Here." She stopped and pressed her bleeding palm against the wall. Again, it opened for her.

Perry pushed her through. "Just keep opening the way ahead. I'll signal the others."

Sienna crossed over the next corridor, trying to tune out the dull thud of fists against flesh, the snarl of the lion and the roaring of the apes behind her. At least there were no screams ... yet. She had to hurry.

The maze began to twist more tightly, the tug inside calling her onwards. After four more walls, she reached a gate made of thick metal bars as tall as the woven branches around it.

"Here. I've found the center!" she called back through the thick walls of the maze. Had they heard her?

Then she saw Mila running through, Perry and the others close behind as they tried to outrun the giant apes.

The gate hung open on its hinges, the lock cracked by whoever had come before them. Sienna darted through and held it open. "Come on!"

Mila rushed through, panting as she tried to catch her breath. Perry and Finn darted ahead of Xander, who lingered as Asada the lion still fought. Sienna could almost feel the adrenalin of the fight through his powerful proxy. Xander's hands were raised, the muscles on his back tense as he drove the lion forward with his will. It savaged the first of the attacking apes as it tried to push through the narrow hedge, ripping into the thick neck. Blood spurted out, and the great ape collapsed, blocking the gap.

The beasts behind bellowed in anger and frustration, but they couldn't pass the wounded body. The lion darted in again, raking at the eyes of the giant ape as if it wanted to tear its face away.

"Come on!" Perry shouted. "Enough. Leave it now, or finish it off."

Xander spun, his eyes fixed on Perry, his face contorted like the lion who stood by his side. Almost as one with his illustrated beast. For a moment, it looked like he would send Asada to rip the other Mapwalker to shreds. Then the wildness left his eyes.

Xander took a breath and slumped forward. He placed the scrap of map leather on the ground, and the lion stalked into it.

Once they were all through, Mila pulled the gate shut and Perry wrapped a little piece of map leather around the broken lock. He conjured just enough flame to fuse the lock closed, so the gate shut firmly behind them.

The sound of the apes faded away as the other beasts moved off.

"There must be another way round," Finn said. "They won't give up."

"Then we better hurry up." Sienna turned to see where they were.

A circle of flat rocks formed a raised platform. In the middle, a pile of charred wood and human bones steamed in the sun.

"It's a pyre," Mila said. "Work of the Shadow Cartographers."

They clambered onto the pyre, the smell of burned wood and roasted flesh intensifying around them. Birds of prey circled above, beady eyes on the carrion below.

Mila used a partially burned branch to rake the pile of burned bones, looking for a sign of what might have happened here.

"You need to look at this, Sienna."

A small round object glinted in the afternoon sun. Sienna looked more closely and realized with a jolt what it was.

Her father's five-pointed compass.

She would recognize it anywhere. Engraved upon the face were the things her father valued, a book, the face of the goddess Aquae Sulis representing Bath, and enclosed within the glass, a lock of her baby hair. Tears welled in Sienna's eyes.

She fell to her knees in the ash. The grey dust billowed around her as she reached for the compass. She wiped it clean to reveal the patterns beneath.

"It's his, isn't it?" Mila said, softly.

Sienna nodded. "He was here." She looked at the pile of bones. "You don't think …?"

Mila shook her head. "He was too valuable to burn. The compass could have been stolen by someone else. These bodies might be rebels or smugglers."

Finn hunkered down to kneel next to Sienna. His closeness comforted her, and she could see a reflection of her loss in his dark eyes. "I know smugglers, and I know rebels. None of them would have left this here when they could get so much for it."

A roar sounded from just outside the gate.

They turned to see the giant apes gathered outside the bars, testing the strength as they eyed the enemy inside. One of the beasts slammed into the metal, its war cry ringing out. The gate shuddered and shook, but it held.

For now.

"We're not getting back out the maze that way," Xander said. "Even if we all fight, we can't hold them off for long. We need another way out of here."

One of the apes started to climb, pulling itself up the gate, hand over hand, baring its yellow teeth as it snarled at them.

Sienna clicked the button at the bottom of the compass, and it flicked open. Inside, the bronze was engraved with his name, John Farren. And on the opposite side, there was a carving, a tiny map inscribed on the inner surface with a castle at its center.

Sienna ran her fingers slowly over the carving, thinking of her father etching these lines. It was rough, but perhaps it was enough. Together with what they had learned before, together with Finn's desire to see his sister and her own to see her father, with Mila's knowledge of where the castle lay. Together they might be able to make it.

First one and then another ape dropped down on their side of the gate. They roared and lumbered towards the team.

"If in doubt ..." Xander said. "Quickly now!"

Sienna's heart thumped as she considered the drip of shadow she would exchange for her blood. But they had no option.

She pulled the scalpel from her bag and used it to cut her hand slightly, dripping blood onto the map in the compass.

It filled the lines, scarlet and gold together with the rays of the sun forming a mesmerizing pool. All she had to do was fly into it.

Sienna felt lightness inside, even though they were surrounded by the stink of beasts with decaying flesh between their teeth, and the burned bones upon which they stood. This was a place of death, and they were going further towards darkness, but she could sense they were almost there. She would see her father again.

"Now would be good," Xander shouted as he turned to face the oncoming charge.

Sienna put one hand around the bloody compass and held her other hand out. The others gripped it and held each other, entwined together as the beasts bore down upon them.

Her heart pounded as she remembered Finn wasn't a Mapwalker. How could he come through? She looked over at him, eyes wide with fear. She didn't want to lose him now.

He nodded back at her. "It's okay, just do your part and I will follow through. And if you make it to the castle without me …" He looked over at Mila. "Then you *will* find my sister and set her free."

Mila nodded. "Quickly now."

Perry hurled a blast of flame, pushing the beasts back. They howled as flame caught fur and one rolled itself into the pile of ash, pieces of bone sticking to its flesh. Then it came for them, a thing of fury and ash, bone and flame.

Sienna closed her eyes, trying to tune out the roar of the beasts, and the expectation of her friends.

She thought of her father, fixing the map from the compass in her mind, and reached for blood in the darkness.

CHAPTER 19

ONE MOMENT SIENNA FELT the sun on her skin and the next it was cold and clammy, the roar of the beasts replaced by quiet water dripping on stone.

"We made it." Finn's voice was filled with wonder.

Sienna opened her eyes to find them in a storage area with a low ceiling and walls of thick stone. They matched the dungeon she and Mila had visited before, and it certainly felt like the same castle. How many of these could there be in the Borderlands?

The sound of voices came from beyond a doorway, and the group melted into the shadows. The voices came closer and then passed by.

"They were talking about taking food up to the women," Finn said, his face set with anger. "I'm going after them."

Mila put a hand on his arm. "Wait a minute. We need to decide what the plan is first."

Finn shook her hand off, spinning towards her, his finger jabbing the air in front of her face.

"I am here for my sister, and you promised to help me."

Mila crossed her arms. "I promised to get you to the castle. I never said we would help you find her and take her home."

Sienna watched the two of them face off. They couldn't

find her father and Finn's sister at the same time, but the Borderlander had risked his life and his future to get here. They wouldn't have made it this far without him, and she couldn't leave him now.

"I'm going with Finn," she said. "We'll find his sister, then we'll come back and together, we'll find my father and the rest of the Extreme Cartographic Force. We won't be long. By the time we come back, you need to be ready to move."

* * *

Finn slipped through the corridor of the castle, Sienna close behind. He was surprised she'd chosen to come along, but he was glad of her help. They followed the servants at a distance through the twisting and turning corridors.

A scream came from up ahead, a primal sound of pain recognizable in any culture as a woman giving birth. Then the scream of a newborn, forced into a world they didn't choose. Finn could smell metallic blood soaked into straw, like an animal's den. He put his hand on the wall to steady himself as thoughts of his sister came to him.

The Shadow Cartographers had come to the citadel, taking those on the edge of womanhood. Isabel had only been fifteen, but already beautiful. She had an edge of magic, a mild gift she used to grow plants in the barren ground of the broken city. But with such a gift, other kinds of magic could be dormant, unlocked if she bred with another.

Finn had heard rumors of what came out of these halls over the years. The Elite Shadow Cartographers, wielding blood magic with precision, creating new worlds from their veins. But also the mutants, those whose magic coalesced into something twisted, tested and found wanting, fodder for sacrifice at the Tophet where the blood of children fueled the dark magic of the mages.

"Are you alright?" Sienna's whisper came from behind him.

Finn pushed away from the wall and nodded, leading her onwards. His heart pounded as he imagined what he might find ahead. Would Isabel even be here? She might be dead from childbirth, or he'd heard the girls who couldn't get pregnant were slaughtered, their blood used in ritual. Useless mouths weren't tolerated here.

He crept forward, peeking around a corner to check the way ahead.

A guard stood in front of a doorway, the edges decorated with horns of plenty, a bountiful harvest and phallic symbols. The fertility halls. A guard paced back and forth in front of the door, alert and ready.

"I'll distract him," Sienna whispered.

Before Finn could stop her, she walked out around the corner towards the guard, hands relaxed by her side. Finn remained in the shadows as the guard turned at her footsteps, his eyes widening at the sight of her. The man leered as Sienna exaggerated the swing of her hips, walking towards him with intent. He gripped the pommel of his sword tighter.

"What are you doing here?" the guard demanded.

Sienna rested against the wall next to him, angling her body so the guard turned, his back to Finn.

"I'm looking for someone." Sienna smiled. "I heard you might be able to help. I'm willing to do whatever it takes to find her." The guard stepped closer, his hand lifting from his sword to caress her cheek. Sienna leaned into him, pressing her body against his.

Finn slipped around the corner, and as the man reached to pull her body closer, Finn brought the pommel of his sword down hard on the back of the guard's head.

A dull thunk and the guard slumped to the ground. Finn would have finished him off, but Sienna stepped over him and bent to pull off the man's belt.

"We'll hogtie him and drag him into the tunnel," she whispered.

They worked quickly and soon had the unconscious guard back in the shadows. By the time he regained consciousness, they'd be long gone.

Sienna looked down at the guard and over at Finn. He felt her eyes appraising him, and he almost blushed under her gaze.

"There'll be more guards inside. It'll be tight, but you'll just fit this uniform."

"No." There was no way he was going to wear such an evil costume and drag Sienna like a captive around this unholy place. "There's too much that could go wrong."

She put her hand on his chest. "I'll be fine, Finn. I won't end up like your sister. We can't get rid of all the guards, so we need to walk unseen. This is the best way."

Finn took a deep breath. He had helped Sienna escape once, and now he felt responsible for her. There was no way he would put her back in danger again, especially here, where women only existed for one thing.

She bent to pull the guard's uniform off. "Help me." When he didn't move, she looked up at him. "Come on, we don't have much time. You want to find Isabel, don't you?"

His sister's name made Finn gasp. It had been so long since he had heard anyone else speak it, for once the girls were taken, they were dead to their families. It was ill-advised to speak of them again, except as the martyred dead. After all, it was an honor to be a vessel for a Halbrasse.

He might be so close to her now.

Finn bent to help Sienna pull off the guard's uniform and swapped his own clothes for the heavy armor of the guard. It shone, freshly polished, with the half-moon of the Shadow Cartographers. He wrapped a piece of rope around Sienna's wrists, tying them behind her back.

"Are you sure it's okay?" He whispered in her ear. "Not too tight?"

He was so close that he could smell the scent of her, a faint vanilla underneath sweat and the blood they had shed together. He had never thought a Mapwalker would look at him the way she did, but it seemed she saw past the external to his inner self.

"Push me ahead of you. Be a little rough. You won't hurt me."

Finn took a deep breath and then pushed Sienna forward a little. "Walk." His voice was stronger now, and he channeled his father as he assumed the swagger of authority.

They walked together into the tangle of winding passages beyond the archway, and as they passed, they peered through the barred windows of each of the cells. One woman lay crumpled on the floor, her body like a broken doll. Another banged on the door, yelling as she pulled at the bars. She screamed at them, pointing at Finn, calling him names Sienna recognized even though the woman spoke in a foreign language. It didn't matter what race you were here, only whether you could breed.

In another cell, a grunting sound and the rhythmic slap of flesh on flesh betrayed what occurred within, as the sound of weeping filled the corridors around them. It was a desolate, ugly place. Finn slowed his steps, wanting to help each one, but there were so many …

Sienna turned, her eyes bright with anger, a flush of red on her cheeks. "We must go on. Your sister might still be here." She looked around her. "We can't help these women one by one. We have to change things at a more fundamental level. And I promise you that we will, Finn. But if we're caught, it's all over. For both of us."

He nodded and as they walked on, the cells changed in nature. Women in different stages of pregnancy paced inside or lay chained on their backs, bellies looming large, closer to term the further they went in.

Then suddenly, there were empty cells. Finn stopped,

looking inside of one, noting the crumpled blanket on the rickety bed, drops of blood on the floor. These women had gone to give birth and then they would be returned to the front cells ready to breed again.

Finn pounded his fist on the door of the last cell. "I'm too late."

A creak came from the end of the corridor.

Sienna slumped to the ground next to Finn's leg in a posture of submission, her head on one side, hair covering her face. A guard walked past, looking over with approval at what he presumed was another man's violent act.

After he passed by, his footsteps fading, Sienna looked towards the door. "There's something else behind there."

Finn took a step towards the door, sweat prickling his back, palms damp with fear of what he might find.

Sienna stood up and walked purposefully towards the door. Finn followed her. She pulled it open and immediately, a stench hit them from within. The smell of emptied bodies, disease and the rot of death. There were several bigger cells back here with up to ten women in each. They were thin and bedraggled, many of them lying on the floor or propped against the walls, some with bloody tunics. They were quiet, resigned to their fate.

"These are the ones they're finished with," Sienna whispered.

Finn frowned. "But some of the women return home. I know one in the Resistance, and she told me that when they've done their duty, they can leave. So why are these women here?"

"Perhaps they have to agree to something?" Sienna wondered aloud. "Maybe the ones who come back have promised to give up others, have promised to send other women. Maybe these are the ones who wouldn't agree."

Finn looked into the first cell, his eyes resting on each of the women in turn, each one a daughter, a mother, perhaps a sister or wife. Each one loved, and yet somehow, they ended up here. He wondered how many looked for them and his heart broke for those women who would never know they were loved. He wished he could help more, but even if they unlocked the doors to let these women out, they would perish on the journey home. They had no strength, and perhaps no will left to survive.

His anger at the Shadow Cartographers rose up inside. They needed to stop this. The only reason to breed Halbrasse was to invade and shift the border into Earth-side. But peace would mean that the Borderlands could develop into a better place. There must be a way. He looked over at Sienna. She wasn't like the other Mapwalkers, she could see both sides. Perhaps she could help.

Finn walked to the next prison door, gazing at each woman in turn. One woman had a shaved head, her face turned to the wall. But the shape of her nose, the set of her mouth were still recognizable.

"Isabel," he whispered.

CHAPTER 20

SOME OF THE WOMEN in the cell looked up with hollow eyes at his voice, but Isabel didn't move. Her chest rose and fell, but it was a faint movement. Her pale skin was almost translucent, and there was blood on her tunic.

"Isabel," he said again, louder this time.

She opened her eyes, and a half-smile played around her mouth as she saw him, but she didn't move, her body too weak.

Finn rattled at the door, but the lock held. Some of the women inside the cell began to moan, calling out to him in different languages. But Finn only had eyes for his sister.

"We need the key," Sienna said, softly. "It's the only way you're going to get to her. I'll stay here, and you go follow the guard."

Finn nodded, reining in his anger. There was no use trying to pick a fight with the guards when he needed to get into the cell as fast as possible. He jogged back down the corridor after the man who had passed them a little while ago.

He walked through into the main section and heard voices down the corridor. Two guards stood outside one of the women's cells. The one who had passed them told a dirty joke as the other man adjusted his uniform, a look of satisfaction on his face. Finn tuned out their words, determined not to get into a fight right now, even though he was desperate to pull out his sword and cut them both into pieces. There was a bunch of keys on the first guard's belt. The men looked up as he approached.

Finn smiled. "Hey there. I need the key for the holding cell in the back section."

The guard looked at him, eyes narrowing. "Haven't seen you around here before."

Finn nodded. "I'm new, just arrived from Old Aleppo with a girl of Mapwalker lineage. You saw her back in the corridor."

The guard nodded. "She looked fresh. Why are you putting her with the rejects?"

Finn sighed, affecting a look of resignation. "I might have sampled the merchandise on the journey, and I promised her a visit with her sister in exchange for her silence. She's a good girl. She'll behave, I promise."

The guard raised his eyebrows and laughed, the hollow noise echoing down the corridor. "Good girl? That's a riot. None of this lot are good, or at least they're only good enough for breeding." He paused, then smiled knowingly. "But we all sample the merchandise, friend. I'll pay her a visit myself later."

The guard shuffled the keys on his belt and pulled off a large brass one. "This will open the holding cells, but bring it back to the guard station as soon as you're done."

Finn took the key, nodded and turned away, walking back down the corridor. As soon as he was out of sight, he clenched his fists and exhaled sharply, pushing down his desire to kill something.

He walked through the final door and put the key in the lock, turning it with a click. As he opened it, some of the women crawled towards him, their arms outstretched as they moaned, asking for pity. Sienna slipped into the room after Finn and began talking to them, her eyes welling with tears.

Finn went to Isabel and pulled her into his arms, leaning back against the wall as he rocked her gently. She was so thin that her bones stuck out through her skin and she smelled of infection.

"It's okay, Izzy. I'm here now, I've come to take you home."

Her eyes flickered open, blue like the sky above the library when they had escaped the darkness of the city together to read in their haven. There was pain in her gaze, a deep suffering from months of torment and grief for what she had lost.

Her lips moved, and Finn bent his head so he could hear her.

"So good to see you." Her voice rasped, the breath of someone shut away from the light for too long.

He pulled out the little horse he had whittled and pushed it into her hand. "I made this for you. She's running like you always wanted to. It's time to run now, Izzy."

"It's too late." Isabel lifted her hand and placed it on her belly over the rust marks of dried blood.

Sienna came over and knelt next to them. She helped Isabel lift her tunic to reveal a deep wound, a yellow and black gash across her stomach oozing with pus and blood, an angry red infection around it. The stench rising from it made Finn gag.

"No," he gasped. "We have to get you out of here."

Isabel put her hand out and held his with the tiny bit of strength she had left.

"This is where we come to die." She took another breath. "But these women did not betray their families. These women are heroes. You have to stop this happening again, Finn. I have a daughter, Emily. Find her. Don't let her be raised by the Shadow Cartographers. Don't let this happen to her."

Tears streamed down Finn's cheeks. "I promise."

Isabel took another breath, and this time there was a rattle as she exhaled. Her head dropped back against Finn's chest, and he held her close as she groaned in pain.

Finn bent his head to hers. "Don't leave me, Izzy."

His sister took one last breath and then she was still.

Her weight sagged against him. His precious sister was lost, and her child was somewhere in this hellhole of a castle. Finn's tears slowed as his anger burned white-hot. He gently laid Isabel's body on the ground, knowing he could not bury her now. This dead flesh was not his sister, and she would want him to find her daughter, not wait here to be taken by the guards.

Finn stood, his body shaking with anger and grief as Sienna closed Isabel's eyes. The women moaned around them, most of them not far off death themselves. Finn clenched his fists and gripped the pommel of his sword. He stormed out of the cell, leaving the door wide open behind him.

"Finn, wait," Sienna shouted after him, but he ignored her. Those guards would be the first to go, and then he would see what other damage he could bring to this evil place.

He ran down the corridor. His blood was up, and he felt like a berserker from the Viking myths he and Izzy read about together. Family and blood were everything.

The two guards turned to face him, their faces confused as he ran towards them. They reached for their weapons, but Finn got there first, bringing his sword down in a heavy swipe cleaving the first man across the belly. He looked down in surprise, hands bloody as he held his stomach. Then his guts slithered out and the man crumpled to the floor.

The other guard pulled his sword and parried Finn, but he was no match for the better swordsman. Finn hacked down his sword, beating the man to his knees.

"Please, take whatever you want."

"I'll take you to Hell." Finn swung his sword, and the man's head separated from his body, rolling to Sienna's feet as she cautiously approached, hands outstretched to pacify him.

"You have to stop now, Finn. There will be more guards coming with all the noise. You can't help Isabel's daughter – your niece – if you're captured."

Sienna came closer, and Finn looked at her, taking in the laughter lines at the corners of her eyes. Laughter seemed so far away right now. He couldn't let her be taken.

"You shouldn't be here." He took her hands in his. "The Borderlands are not your place. I wouldn't wish this life on anyone, and certainly not on you." He slowly lifted a finger to stroke her cheek. He wanted to kiss her, to lose himself in her.

The sound of running feet and the shouts of guards came from the corridors ahead.

Finn grabbed Sienna's hand. "We need to get back to the others, find your father and Emily."

He took one last look at the cells behind, the women trapped inside. He would avenge his sister, and then he would stop this evil trade. He would find whoever ran this place and bring it down. If it took him the rest of his life.

Together, they ran back through the corridors, down to the storeroom where the others waited.

Mila looked up as they came in, noting the blood on Finn's clothes. "What the hell?"

"Finn's sister is dead," Sienna said. "But he has a niece, and there are more children here, born from enforced slavery."

Finn stepped forward. "You need to find Sienna's father, but I'm going after the children. I wish you all the best for your journey onwards."

He nodded at them all. At the door, he took one last look back at Sienna, wondering if he would ever see her again. She would soon be returning Earth-side, and his path was here in the Borderlands. He turned and walked out of the door.

* * *

Sienna watched Finn go. What she had seen in the fertility halls had shocked her to the core. Like him, she wanted to free all the women, tear down this hated castle. But there weren't enough of them to win the war now. She had to find her father first, but she swore to return here. She could only hope that Finn would make it. He had fulfilled his part of the bargain, and now, of course, he had to try to save his family. But her heart ached as he walked out and she suddenly realized the Borderlander meant more than she had thought. Their little team was incomplete without him.

"We did some investigating," Mila said, interrupting her thoughts. "The dungeons where we saw the flesh maps are another level down."

Sienna nodded her head. "Let's go." Her voice was strong, but inside she wondered whether her father could possibly still be alive.

As they walked down the corridor and descended the stairs to the level of the dungeons, a sense of foreboding rose inside her. A copper smell of dried blood hung in the air mingled with smoke from torches held in brackets against the wall.

They heard the sound of running feet as they walked, but all were heading away from them. Finn's rampage had drawn the guards away from them and Sienna hoped that somehow he would be able to escape.

They came to a partially open door. Sienna pushed it open to find a man, or what had once been a man, chained face down on a thick wooden table. His back had been carved with the lines of a city, his ruined flesh still wet with blood. His hair was matted and stuck to his head, his face turned away. But the shape of his shoulders, the curve of his neck were familiar. Could it possibly be him?

CHAPTER 21

"CAREFUL." MILA WALKED IN beside Sienna. Perry and Xander followed behind, keeping an eye out for the guards.

The room was dimly lit by the flicker of flames in a stone fireplace and torches in brackets around the walls. Rushes covered the floor by the table, dark with blood.

Sienna walked to the man's head. With a shaking hand, she gently pulled back the hair around his face. Her hand flew to her mouth and tears welled in her eyes as she saw his features. His eyes were shut and swollen from a beating, his lips cracked and bleeding, but it was her father.

"Dad," she whispered, kneeling next to him, her fingers brushing his temple. His body must be a mass of agony, and yet somehow he still lived.

The man's eyes flickered open, a piercing blue, and when he saw her a flash of recognition lit up his face and then a deep despair came over him.

"Sienna," he whispered. "You shouldn't be here."

"I came to take you home." She looked around desperately for a way to get him out of the bonds. Perry and Mila searched the room for a way to unlock the shackles. Xander stood by the door, his body tense and alert.

"Here." Mila held up a key and then returned to the

table, unlocking the shackles at John's wrists and ankles. He groaned, flinching as he arched away from the wood. Blood ran from the wounds on his back, revealing the city in more detail.

Mila's eyes widened. "It's Old Aleppo." Her eyes met Sienna's. "They're drawing the city of the warlord into Earthside. They're going to shift the Borderlands."

John nodded. "My skin is the Map of Shadows. They lured us here –" His words were cut off as he coughed, blood trickling from the side of his mouth.

Perry and Sienna helped John sit up, his face a mask of agony as he tried to speak again. "They needed more power, a map made from the skin of a Blood Cartographer, a map that would remake the border in their favor and start the invasion."

He paled, eyes closing as his head lolled to one side.

"No, Dad, please," Sienna whispered as his body slumped against hers.

Perry helped her lift him, blood soaking into his shirt. "Usually the Blood Cartographers are tattooed over a long period of time, often slowly for years." He frowned. "This has been done in a hurry. Each drop of his blood makes the map stronger, but it may cost him everything."

"We have to get him back to the Ministry."

John's eyes fluttered open. "Don't let them use my body, Sienna. Destroy the map. Finish me so they can't use it." He reached out a hand in desperation.

Sienna took it in hers. "You're coming home with me." Tears welled in her eyes, and she thought of Finn losing Isabel, and of the skins in the nearby dungeon. Was this land only one of loss, a dark reflection of the world she had left behind? "I need you, Dad. Besides, I don't know how to get us all home. I need you to show me."

John's head dropped again, his eyes rolling back in his head as he passed out.

"We need to get him to a doctor," Sienna said.

Mila looked grave. "The only way is to get him back to the Ministry. Can you take us all through?"

Sienna nodded. "I'll try." But in her heart, she worried that she wasn't strong enough.

Suddenly from outside the door came the double-time step of a patrol heading towards them.

"Shut the door, Xander," Mila called. "You can't let them in. Sienna will be able to get us all out of here soon enough."

Xander turned, and his face was as Sienna had glimpsed it in the jungle and again in the torture of the beasts in the labyrinth. His hazel-gold eyes were now black.

"I don't think so." Xander's voice was quiet, and he stepped aside as a group of guards arrived. They filed into the room, weapons pointed at the team, forming a phalanx of sharp spears. Xander stood with them facing the Mapwalker team.

Footsteps echoed down the hall and a tall man walked in, a wolf pelt cloak over his tailored suit.

Perry did a double take, his face a mask of confusion. "Dad?"

Sienna recognized Sir Douglas Mercator, the man who tried to buy her grandfather's map shop. Cartographic royalty and it would seem – a Shadow Cartographer.

"Good to see you all." Sir Douglas smiled. "Especially you, son. This map –" He pointed at John. "Is the last map we need before the invasion." He inclined his head towards Sienna. "And her blood will help make it more powerful."

Perry shook his head. "No, I didn't bring her for that." Perry looked over at Sienna and Mila, shaking his head. "I didn't know, I promise."

"But I did." Xander stepped forward,

"Why are you doing this?" Mila said, her fists clenched. Sienna put a hand on her arm to hold her friend's anger back.

"It's time for a change," Xander answered. "I'm sick of hiding our magic as we do Earth-side, pretending we are nothing. Here in the Borderlands, I can use my powers as much as I like. I can create anything. My future lies here."

Sir Douglas put his hand on Xander's shoulder, nodding his head with pride. "You've done well." He looked over at Perry. "And now you, my son. It's time to stand with us. The balance is shifting. You can embrace who you truly are, a Halbrasse of great power."

"But … I can't –"

"That man killed Morwenna." Sir Douglas spat the words as he pointed at John. "He murdered your mother."

"No." Sienna turned to Perry, pleading with them. "There must be some mistake or a reason why. Please –"

Perry looked over at John and hung his head, his body crumpling in on itself, defeated. The guards took a step forward, weapons threatening, faces set with a lust for blood.

But Perry's head snapped up as they moved towards his friends.

He reached into the fireplace behind him and pulled out a burning coal, holding in front with a shaking hand. It burned with ferocity. "Don't come any closer."

Sir Douglas put a hand out to stop the guards. They halted, weapons drawn, ready to charge on his word.

"Don't fight this, son. These three are nothing to you. We can use the skin of the two Blood Cartographers to create even more powerful maps, and the girl of water will go to the breeding room. Perhaps her magic will combine to produce a powerful child."

"I'll take her as part of my reward," Xander said, his eyes raking down Mila's body.

Mila spat at him. "I wouldn't come anywhere near you."

"No one said you had a choice. I take what's mine." Xander pulled his map from his pocket and placed it on the ground. This time, instead of the lion, Asada, a hybrid beast emerged, one created from his sketches along the journey. It had the powerful limbs of the giant ape, rising to the height of the ceiling, but it had scales and a snout like a dragon and when it opened its jaws to roar, its teeth were razor sharp.

Perry took a step back.

Sir Douglas smiled with a look of triumph. "It's over. Join us, Sienna. Use your blood willingly for the Map of Shadows, for real power, or I will bleed it from you as I have from your father."

Mila took a step closer to Sienna and put her hand out. Sienna took it, and they stood in front of John's body together, Perry by their side.

Sir Douglas shook his head at their defiance. "Then it's over." He dropped his hand. The guards and the hybrid beast started forward.

Perry threw the burning coal down to the floor in front of them and stepped back behind it, concentrating his power. Fire burst from the coal, and a wall of flame rose up between them and their attackers.

"Don't be stupid, son," Sir Douglas shouted over the crackling of the flames. "End this now and join me."

Perry reached out his hands, urging the flames higher, feeding off the coals in the grate. The hybrid beast screeched as it tried to push through, its dragon scales protecting it but the great ape limbs burned. The stench of singed flesh filled the room. Xander urged it on, his face contorted with anger. "Attack!"

"Hurry," Perry called back to Sienna, his body taut with the effort of commanding the flames. "I can't hold them too long."

Mila and Sienna dragged John's body back to the stone wall behind the flames.

John's eyes flickered open. "I don't have long, Sienna. Leave me here to burn and get away. Please."

"It's no use," Xander called over the flames. "Even if you go back, it will be too late. When I repaired the rent Michael made in the border, I left a back door. The warlord of Old

Aleppo will be entering Bath even now, and your rebel friend won't be there to stop him this time. The Ministry is finished, so you have nothing to go back for." He held up a small rolled-up parchment. "And besides, I have your star map, Sienna. You're trapped here."

* * *

Finn ran through the castle corridors, glancing into rooms as he passed, trying to see where they might keep the children. He came upon a couple of guards playing dice in a murky side room. They looked up as he entered, faces guilty at being caught before changing to alarm as Finn reached for his sword, shutting the door behind him.

A swift slash and one of the guards lay gurgling on the ground, clutching at his bloody throat. The other backed away, hands outstretched in supplication.

"Please, what do you want? I can help you."

Finn stalked towards the cowering man. "Where are the Halbrasse children kept?"

The man paled. "I ... You can't –"

Finn pointed at the now-dead guard. "You want to join him?"

The man slumped. "The children are held in the east wing. There are dormitories and a school where they learn to use their abilities." He shook his head. "But none of us go there. We don't need to. They guard themselves."

"Which way?"

"Follow the corridor to the end and then cross the courtyard into the east wing. It has its own door."

Finn leaned in and thumped the man on the side of the head with the pommel of his sword. The guard collapsed on the floor, unconscious. Finn turned and walked out of the storeroom, hurrying east.

He reached a wide courtyard, open to the sky above. It was dark and Finn could see the stars above, a serenity that calmed his pounding heart. He looked up at the tower in front of him, a huge wooden door the final barrier to the children's wing.

It was strangely quiet. The rest of the castle had plenty of guards but there seemed to be none here. He walked around the edge of the courtyard, staying in the shadows in case anyone was watching. But it was silent except for his quiet footsteps on the gravel.

The hair on the back of his neck prickled as he reached the door. It was carved with the half-moon of the Shadow Cartographers.

He pushed it open, and it creaked on heavy hinges. As Finn stepped inside, he heard the rustle of clothes and the giggle of children. There was a lamp further down the hall, but it was semi-darkness by the door. He caught a glimpse of little shadows moving around, hiding behind the furniture.

"Hello," Finn whispered. "Anybody here?"

A giggle to his right and he turned to see a little girl peeking out from behind a chair. She wore a white nightdress, and her blonde hair was tied in two pigtails.

"Hi there." Finn knelt down and smiled, stretching out his hand towards her. "I'm Finn, a friend. I'm not going to hurt you."

Soft footsteps echoed in the corridor, and he looked up to see a group of children coming towards him, the littlest toddling along holding hands with an older child. They were angelic in the moonlight streaming through the high windows, all of them in white nightgowns, all different races, a picture of the diversity of the Borderlands.

But as they drew closer, he could see their faces weren't welcoming. They weren't scared. They were ready to attack.

The first little boy pointed at Finn. "Stranger," he whispered, softly at first.

They all joined in. "Stranger. Stranger." Marching towards

him, fingers outstretched, voices growing louder as they approached. "Stranger."

Finn held his hands out wide. "It's okay. I'm not here to hurt you. I'm –"

The blow came from nowhere.

A sudden burning explosion in his side and Finn fell sideways with the force of it. He cried out in pain, looking at the little girl by the chair. She had one hand out, her head tilted sideways as she looked at him.

"Stranger," she said along with the others and blasted him again. A ball of fire leapt from her fingers and smashed into Finn. He flew backwards, hitting the wall behind him. The smell of burning metal came from his body armor. He wouldn't last long against her onslaught.

The march of little feet came closer, the children's chanting getting louder as they approached, hands held out ready to attack.

CHAPTER 22

FINN GRIPPED THE POMMEL of his sword, but he couldn't bring himself to attack or even threaten the children. They didn't know what they were and they had been taught to hate. There was no chance of finding Emily now, and if he stayed, they would kill him.

He took one last look at the children and then scrambled back towards the door.

"Stranger." The little girl blasted him again, and Finn was knocked sideways, banging his head against the metal rivets. He pulled himself on, legs like jelly from the attack as he hauled himself out of the door. He rolled back into the courtyard, lying on the gravel, panting with pain. If they came out now, they would finish him.

But the door slammed shut, and he was left alone, staring up at the stars.

Finn lay there for a moment, his breath returning to normal as the pain eased. It was like the little girl had electrocuted him. What the hell kind of power did she have? He had heard Mila say that every use of magic in the Borderlands meant a little more shadow in the Mapwalker who used it. But what did that mean for these little Halbrasse? His niece, Emily, was only a newborn so it would be years before her talents could be exploited.

He had time – but he needed the help of the Mapwalkers. He needed Sienna. The others were already set in their prejudice against the Borderlanders, but she had seen a different side of his people. She was hope for a shared future.

Finn rolled over and pushed himself up onto his knees, then staggered to his feet. His whole body felt weak with the aftermath of the attack, but he had to get back to Sienna before she mapwalked back to Earth-side. He might never have this chance again.

* * *

Sienna heard Xander's words through the roar of the flames. She looked at Mila, saw in her eyes that it could be true, that he could have left a gap in the border ready to be exploited when the time was right. She remembered the fetish map she'd seen in the first visit to the dungeons of the castle, where Bath lay broken, a burnt-out shell, its inhabitants slaughtered by feral invaders.

"We have to get back." She looked at her father. "And we're not leaving anyone behind."

Sienna's mind raced as she considered the star map Xander held. It was supposedly the only reliable way to get home, to orientate across the border, but she had created a map from nothing before. She had to do it again.

She turned to Perry. "Can you hold them a little longer?"

He grimaced, his face ruddy from the flames and she saw the flicker of shadow in his eyes. There was a chance he had used too much magic in a short time, that he would tip over to his father's side, but she had to believe he would hold the line.

"For Galileo," he said, steel in his voice.

Sienna took the scalpel from her bag and cut into her arm. As blood welled, she closed her eyes and began to sketch the lines of Bath on the stone wall in front of her. She tuned out the throb of pain, the roar of the beast and the flames at her back. She fixed her imagination on the city she had only just begun to know, the map shop on the little street with the coffee shop opposite, Mila's canal boat and Zippy waiting alongside, the Abbey and the Baths. She painted them on the wall with her blood, and as she drew it, she felt a tug towards home, the pull of the map.

Her father looked up, and Sienna saw pride mixed with fear in his eyes. Fear, not for himself, but for her future now he saw what she could do. But there was no time to think about what might happen. They had to go.

Beyond the fire, the guards redoubled their efforts, thrusting long pikes through the flames towards Perry. Sir Douglas shouted something, and one of them ran through, bellowing his rage.

Perry blasted a stream of flame at him, and the guard tottered forward, his body alight. He slammed into the wooden table, flames consuming his body, but the height of the main wall ebbed a little with the distraction.

Xander urged his great beast forward, and it reached through the flames, screaming as it lit afire, but this time, it kept coming.

Perry fell back as it advanced. "We need to get out of here."

Sienna placed her hands on the wall, letting her mind sink into the lines, opening the portal back to the shop, back to where the rustle of her grandfather's maps called her.

Mila dragged John towards the wall, ready to cross over behind her. Perry edged back, trying to keep the beast far enough away but still ready to join them.

"Sienna!" Finn's voice suddenly came across the flames.

She turned to see him dart into the room, slashing at the guards as he moved towards the wall of flame. The beast lunged for him, but he rolled underneath it, angling his sword across its belly, cutting it deeply as he sprang away on the other side.

For a moment, Sienna faltered, the intensity of the map fading as she was drawn back towards Finn. If they left him, he would certainly be killed. But he couldn't cross into Earth-side, could he?

"Go now," Mila urged. "We have to."

Sienna took one last look back at Finn, as he fought with two guards on the other side of the wall of flame. She opened the map again, felt the expansion of the world beneath her.

She reached out her hands, touching Perry with one and her father with the other, felt Mila's hand on her arm and closed her eyes.

"No!"

Sienna opened her eyes to see Finn dart through the flames just as they died out – as Perry grasped her hand – as the guards surged forward with a roar – as the beast stormed at them, jaws gaping wide.

Finn reached out his arm and wrapped it around Sienna's waist. She buried her head against his chest as she took them through the map.

* * *

The air cooled, and the sound of chaos abated. It smelled of parchment and the faint tang of ink. Sienna opened her eyes to find them all back in the map shop, her father on the floor, Mila at his side, Perry dazed from the fight as he sat down, his face pale from the exertion of using so much magic.

Sienna stood wrapped in Finn's arms, feeling the beating of his heart against her body. She rested there, safe in his arms, a moment of calm after the escape.

Sienna looked up at him. "You're here."

Finn smiled, his dark eyes betraying his wonder. "You can bring Borderlanders across."

"It's only because the border is open right now." Mila stood up and brushed the ash from her clothes. She looked over at Finn. "You'd be gone otherwise, lost in whatever darkness holds our two worlds apart."

Sienna pulled away from him. "I'm sorry. I didn't know."

Finn shook his head. "You couldn't have stopped me trying to come after you."

Mila opened the door. The night was calm, just the sounds of friendly banter from the pub down the road and the soft patter of rain against the windows. For a moment, it seemed as if everything was normal.

Then they heard the howl of a wolf … and screaming.

"They've broken through," Mila said. "I need to get down to The Circus. The Ministry team will be there, or at least on their way. We need to shut the Gate, so the Borderlanders are sucked back through."

Finn gripped the pommel of his sword. "I'm coming too. You need someone to watch your back, and it's my father out there. I know how he works."

Mila nodded and then looked down at John, broken and bleeding on the floor, then over at Perry, collapsed against one of the map cabinets. "You need to get to the Ministry, Sienna. Get to the Blood Gallery and renew the lines of the border. Your blood is powerful, and you can send them back. Bridget will show you how."

Sienna bent down to her father and stroked the matted hair back from his forehead. His chest rose and fell in a jerky movement, but he still lived. He needed medical help, but there would be no chance if the city fell. She clenched her fists. She would not lose her father again.

"I'll renew the lines, and then I'll come and help you close that Gate."

She looked up at Finn and met his eyes. His gaze softened,

and then he nodded. Sienna took hold of her father and Perry and traveled into the map of Bath, her mind fixed on the Ministry below the Abbey.

* * *

Finn watched Sienna fade, marveling at the magic of Mapwalking.

"Let's go, lover boy," Mila snapped as she darted out of the map shop into the rain. Finn headed after her, and as he emerged into the night, he couldn't help but stare at the buildings around him. His home in Old Aleppo was broken and crumbling, a shade of its former glory, but this city was intact, its buildings commanding the eye with beautiful stone facades. Flowers bloomed in window boxes, and as they passed a shop on the end, Finn gaped to see paintings of the ocean and sculptures of birds. This was a place where people made art, a city of life, not death, and he desperately wanted more of it. Could the Borderlands ever be like this?

A woman screamed and ran past the end of the road. A huge grey wolf loped behind, barreling into her and taking her down, its teeth sinking into the flesh of her neck, cutting off her scream as the beast shook her.

Finn ran forward, swinging his sword in a low arc, using the flat of the blade to smash into the wolf's face, sending it twisting away. It let the woman go, and she lay unmoving on the ground. The creature turned and snarled, slinking back towards them. Finn stood in front of the woman's body, sword raised, ready to fight, Mila beside him.

Then deep growls came from the shadows in every direction. The wolf pack surrounded them.

"I've got this," Mila said. She held out her hands to the rain, and where the water touched her skin, she rippled with power as she channeled the element. She began to spin one hand, whirling the drops into a tornado of water and then spun it out like a whip at the nearest wolf.

It smashed the beast backwards, lifting it against the stone wall behind. It fell limp to the ground. Mila whirled the tornado on, using it to send the wolves flying away. With two more badly injured, the others slunk off, running off to find easier prey.

"Nicely done," Finn said, hefting his sword.

"We're not done yet. We have to get to the center of that." Mila pointed down the road towards a dense mist forming around The Circus.

A few Borderlanders staggered out of it, disorientated by the buildings around them, mouths gaping open as if they couldn't believe what they saw around them. "Looks like the full force hasn't come through yet."

Then the beating of drums came from within the mist, a rhythmic pounding that echoed through the streets.

"War drums," Finn said. "My father is coming."

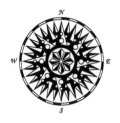

CHAPTER 23

A RUSH OF COOL air touched her skin and Sienna opened her eyes to find herself surrounded by the skins of the Blood Gallery, her father and Perry slumped at her feet. The flesh here was respectfully displayed and honored as a critical part of the Ministry, but in the end, they were still skin maps etched with the blood of people like her father.

And herself.

For a moment, all she could hear was their breathing. Then the sound of a blaring alarm rang out within the Ministry. The attack must have started.

John groaned, and Sienna leaned down to brush his hair from his face. She shuddered to think that he had almost ended up in the Blood Gallery of the Shadow Cartographers.

The door opened with a creak.

"Sienna?" Bridget came through the door, followed by one of her clerks. She looked down at the two men on the floor. "John?" She turned to the clerk. "Get the medics down here."

The man rushed back out, and Bridget came to kneel by her friend. John's blood had dried a little, but he was still a mess of cut and bruised flesh, barely recognizable.

Bridget put out a hand on his arm, lightly touching the skin between his wounds. "You're home now, my love," she whispered, tears welling in her eyes, then she looked up. "Where are Mila and Xander?"

Sienna quickly filled Bridget in, and the Irish woman's eyes darkened as she heard of Xander's betrayal.

"We have to strengthen the borders again and close the Gate." Bridget looked at Sienna. "Are you ready?"

Three medics burst through the door, two carrying a stretcher. Between them, they rolled John gently onto the support and carried him out, the other man supporting Perry as they headed out to the Ministry hospital.

Bridget turned to Sienna as the door closed behind them. "John is strong, he should make it through, but he can't help us now. We have to do this together. We are the only Blood Cartographers left now, but we do have the help of one who loved you very much." She walked to a circular wooden table set in the middle of the room.

Sienna frowned as she approached it, suddenly seeing the new skin mounted there, the edges pegged out so the torso and limbs could be clearly seen. The leather was wrinkled and tanned in parts, but the tattoos were finely drawn, the lines of the ancient city of Bath visible with the Borderlands beyond.

Then she realized whose skin it was.

Sienna's hand flew to her mouth. "Grandfather," she whispered. Nausea rushed over her, and she clutched at her throat. "No."

Bridget put out a hand. "It's what Michael wanted. It's why he inked himself like this. His skin and his blood magic helped define and strengthen the border here. He lived to protect it, and in death, he protects it still. But because Xander left a back door, it needs fresh blood, Sienna. It has to be yours." Bridget hung her head. "My blood magic is weak now, I've used it too much in recent times and the shadow has grown strong in me. I … I feel its dark pull."

"I felt a glimmer of it in the Borderlands," Sienna said,

stepping closer to the table. "It was powerful, like the edge of addiction."

Bridget nodded. "Yes, and the feeling will grow every time you use your magic. If I use mine now, I'm afraid I won't be strong enough. It will pull me too far into the shadow side, and they will win."

Bridget picked up the ritual knife from beside the map and held it out. "This was Michael's. Blood Cartographers have used it for generations, and I know he would have wanted you to have it now."

She held it out towards Sienna.

* * *

The rhythmic thump of drums beat through Finn's chest. The deep notes echoed within him, bringing back memories of joining his father on raids at the edge of the Uncharted where they would gather slaves to sell to the Shadow Cartographers. Slave women he now knew became forced vessels for the Halbrasse, and men they used for sacrifice to the gods of the once dead.

The warlord's men would drink a special concoction before forming their ranks, downing a sharp alcohol spiked with hallucinogenic plants and flavorful herbs. It gave them an edge in battle, a belief that they were superhuman in strength and power. It made them uncaring of physical pain, separating their rational minds from willing bodies. These were the men who would cross into Earth-side through the gathered mist, a vanguard for the warlord's hand-picked warriors.

Finn ran down the road towards The Circus as tendrils of mist stretched further out from the great plane trees in the center.

"Wait," Mila shouted after him. "We need backup."

"No time," Finn called back. Up ahead, he could see a gathering crowd of tourists and locals, staring with interest at the mist, some with devices they held up to capture images of the strange sight. The wolves were running in the side streets, but here, people were entranced, unheeding of the danger.

"Move away from the area," a police officer shouted, waving people back as he stood on the edge of the mist.

Suddenly, a huge axe came out of the grey above him, hacking into the man's shoulder, cleaving his arm away. The officer dropped to his knees as the attacker emerged, face tattooed with the half-moon, teeth bared in a bloody grimace. The crowd backed away in horror and turned to run, tripping over each other, screaming as they tried to escape.

The Borderlander launched into a flurry of death-dealing blows, wielding the axe in a frenzied, drug-fueled state.

Finn didn't falter, he ran straight at the axe-man, swinging his sword as he approached from behind. He thrust his weapon into the man's back, angling the sharp blade so it pierced the man's heart, tugging him closer with a neck hold as the murderer died. Then Finn pushed the body forward, pulling his blade out.

"Run!" he bellowed at the people still there. Those remaining ran or crawled away as Finn picked up the man's fallen axe and turned to face the swirling mist.

The drums beat faster.

Mila stood by Finn's side, her hands lifted to the falling rain as she called it to her, twisting the water into tornado whips. The mist parted, and a horde of Borderlanders strode through in filed ranks. These were not the Ferals those on Earth-side talked of, these were the warriors of the warlord of Old Aleppo come to take what was rightfully theirs. They were dressed in the cast-off, mismatched uniforms of dead soldiers, those who slipped through the border, but they walked in unison.

They were an army.

In the middle of the men, Finn saw his father. Kosai held up a hand to halt the company. His soldiers stood to attention, eyes fixed forward, disciplined enough not to break ranks when faced with this strange environment.

"Have you come to welcome me, son?" The warlord walked forward. "Or beg for mercy after you took what was mine?" He looked Mila up and down, lingering on the curves of her body. "Have you brought me tribute?"

Finn lifted his weapons and took a fighting stance.

The soldiers either side immediately stepped forward, swords raised, blocking his path to their warlord.

Kosai laughed and shook his head. "Do you think you can stop this, Finn? It is beyond time that we took Earthside for our home." He turned around, his arms raised as he looked up at the stunning architecture. "Look at this place. Wouldn't you rather live here than in the ruins of Old Aleppo or in one of their cast-off forgotten cities?"

"There are people here already," Finn said, his voice controlled.

Kosai spun round, eyes blazing with anger. "People who will take our place in the Borderlands. People who deserve to suffer for what they have done to those of us pushed out of this earth." His voice softened. "Join me, son. Rule with me in this new world, and help me build a better life for *our* people."

Finn thought of the castle and Isabel's death, the way Sienna had helped him, the possibilities for a future where both sides of the border could be better somehow. He sighed. "I know the Mapwalkers on this side will help us. If you would just talk with them, Father, I –"

"Take them." Kosai's voice cut off Finn's words and the guards either side swarmed in, blocking Finn's blows and taking him swiftly to the ground. Mila spun out a tornado whip, cutting one of the soldiers down but then she too was overcome.

"I can't trust you, Finn. You've clearly spent too much time with these lying Earth-siders." Kosai nodded to the men. "Hold him."

Two of the biggest guards forced Finn to his knees. Another pulled his head back, exposing his throat to the warlord.

"You were my son once," Kosai said, "but now you will be the first sacrifice to Moloch on Earth-side soil for thousands of years, the first of many offered in the days to come as Borderlanders take all of it back."

"No!" Mila shouted. The man holding her wrapped an arm around her neck, choking her into silence.

The warlord smiled. "Don't worry, beautiful. We won't take your head. You're going to the breeding rooms of the Halbrasse." He turned back to Finn. "But this one …"

Kosai pulled a knife from his belt and stepped closer to his son.

* * *

Sienna looked at the ritual knife in Bridget's outstretched hand. It had an ivory blade bound with a leather strap tied into a series of knots around the end. The border had to be closed, but she couldn't bring herself to touch it.

She looked down at her grandfather's skin, trying to equate the tanned leather with the living man she once knew. This was the fate her father had tried to keep her from, because he would eventually hang in this gallery … and so would she.

But if she ran from the Ministry now, she would find a changed city, and the border could be redrawn in other places too.

Sienna reached out and took the ritual knife. "What do I do?"

"Your blood knows its power," Bridget said. "Just let it out."

Sienna cut into her arm, letting ruby drops drip onto her grandfather's skin. Bridget used a fine brush to paint it over the lines of the ancient city, the circle and the half-moon of The Circus and Royal Crescent, down to the Abbey and around the Baths, along the border around the city.

As her blood sank into the leather, Sienna felt a pulsing as if her heart beat inside the city itself. Screams echoed in her mind as the shadows began to be sucked back inside the border.

* * *

The earth shook, and the warlord stumbled, his knife slicing to one side as he was thrown off balance, hitting one of his own men with a glancing blow.

"What the –?"

Finn took his chance and rolled out of the grip of the men holding him, springing to one side, grabbing the blade from one of the soldiers. He turned swiftly, slicing the man's throat.

Mila ducked under the arm of the man who held her, clawing the rain down into a whip and then spinning it around her, cutting through the soldiers as they looked about in horror.

A howl came from the shadowed streets, the animal sound of beasts in pain. The soldiers fell from their tight formation as the mist swirled about them, the ground shaking as they began to be sucked back into the vortex of the gate.

"The border is closing," Mila shouted in triumph. "Sienna must have made it!"

Finn heard her words and despair shot through him, for it meant that he must go too. He couldn't be on this side when the gate finally shut, or he would dissipate into shadow, and somehow, he had to see Sienna again.

The soldiers scattered, some going willingly back into the mist. Others tried to run, but tendrils of grey reached out for them, dragging them back into the copse of trees and then through the Shadow Gate.

The warlord stood, legs akimbo, bracing himself against the moving earth. He looked at Finn. "This isn't over. I'll be waiting for you on the other side."

He strode back into the mist.

* * *

Bridget looked at Sienna. "The gate must be closed properly, so you need to go back up to The Circus. The Ferals will be swept back through as the border closes and you can use your blood to seal it."

Finn.

Sienna thought of the last look they had shared, the things that remained unsaid. She had to get to him.

"I'll go right now." She picked up the ritual knife and laid her hand on her grandfather's skin. A pulse arced where she touched it and she smiled to think of some part of him wishing her well. She closed her eyes and used the map to travel to The Circus, lifting away in her mind.

* * *

She opened her eyes to find herself in the Georgian circular terrace, but instead of pristine pavements, injured and dying Borderlanders, tourists and police littered the streets. Two wolves tore at one body, ripping chunks of flesh as they worried at it with bloody jaws even as they were sucked back towards the vortex of the mist. The smell of death lingered in the air, and the fetid stench of the Borderlands swirled in the mist around her.

But it receded even as she watched, slowly swirling back towards the copse of plane trees, circling the gate between them.

Was she too late?

Sienna ran into the mist. "Finn!"

Tears ran down her cheeks as she tore into the grey, clammy air sticking to her skin as she tried to see through the shadows to where he might be.

The circle of trees emerged, and suddenly she saw him. He stood next to one of the great plane trees, right on the edge of the border. The mist chased at her heels, and she knew that as soon as it disappeared, the border would go too, the gate would close, and he would be sucked into the darkness.

"Sienna!"

She ran into his arms, and Finn pulled her close, dipping his head down to meet her lips. They clung to one another, lost in a kiss where borders meant nothing.

The wind picked up around them. Sienna pulled away. "I'll come to you. I'll find you again."

Finn took a deep breath and walked towards the shadow gate. As the mist swirled closer, he turned and looked at her, an unspoken promise in his eyes.

Then he stepped through.

As the last of the mist dissipated into the air, Sienna drew the knife along her arm once more. With tears running down her cheeks, she used her blood to paint ancient runes on the trees, following the lines her grandfather had carved before her.

EPILOGUE

Two days later.

SIENNA SAT AT THE old desk in the map shop, her grand-father's parchment in front of her portraying the ancient city of Bath. The oversize globe sat next to her, in pride of place at her right hand, a reminder of how borders had shifted over time. The door to the shop was open, and the smell of freshly roasted coffee came from the café over the road. A light breeze whispered across the maps with a rustle.

The sounds and smells of normality.

Sienna breathed a sigh of relief. Her father recovered in the Ministry hospital, his back healing from his physical wounds even as he drifted in and out of consciousness, muttering of nightmares. On Bridget's urging, Sienna hadn't told her mother about what had happened or about John being back. That was one conversation she would tackle when her father was ready. If he ever was.

Perry was back in the chambers of the Ministry, practicing his fire magic with newfound confidence, driving flames into his targets again and again. Sienna knew he saw Xander's face there alongside his father's and she had no doubt that Perry would want to be on the next mission into the Borderlands. Mila had taken her canal boat east, escaping onto the water, Zippy by her side as she recovered in her own way.

Sienna had no way of knowing what had happened to Finn after the border closed. She could only hope that he had joined the underground Resistance and escaped Old Aleppo, away from the wrath of his father.

She picked up the fountain pen and began to trace over the lines of central Bath with deep red ink, new drops of her blood mingling with her grandfather's. Each stroke of the pen was a line of power, strengthening the border as she traced the arch of the Royal Crescent, the straight line of Brock Street and the curves of The Circus.

For now, the border was closed again, and Finn's world was separate from hers. But Sienna was counting the hours until she could go back into the Borderlands again. She remembered the other blood maps in the castle dungeon, the world remade. The Shadow Cartographers had many more plans, and one setback would not stop them.

Before Bath, Sienna had been drifting through life, unable to see the path ahead. But now she would make her own map and this was only the beginning.

ENJOYED MAP OF SHADOWS?

Thanks for joining Sienna and the Mapwalker team in *Map of Shadows*. If you enjoyed the book, a review would be much appreciated as it helps other readers discover the story.

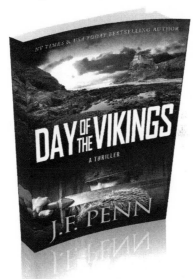

Get a free copy of the bestselling thriller, *Day of the Vikings*, an ARKANE thriller, when you sign up to join my Reader's Group. You'll also be notified of giveaways, new releases, including the next Mapwalker book, and receive personal updates from behind the scenes of my books.

Click here to get started:

www.JFPenn.com/free

AUTHOR'S NOTE

I hope you enjoyed this fantasy as an escapist story, but perhaps you also glimpsed something of the themes beneath as you read. Here's how the idea came into being.

I moved to Bath, England, in 2015 and discovered an antique map shop in a little pedestrianized street between the Royal Crescent and The Circus. I walked past it almost every day when I went to the café to write, and one day, I went in and bought some books. It sparked my research around cartography, maps, and the obsession that humans seem to have with finding our physical place in the world.

Bath can seem perfect at times, with its Roman Baths, medieval Abbey, Georgian architecture and tasteful shops and restaurants. I love living here, but the darker edge of my imagination invented a shadow side to the city, a place just off the edge of the map, and the Borderlands were born.

In November 2016, we visited Israel on a research trip for my ARKANE thriller, *End of Days*. Borders are a big deal in Israel, surrounded as it is by nations who want to destroy it, and split internally by occupied territory. When we traveled to the West Bank, through checkpoints that Palestinians couldn't cross, I began to think about what it meant to be born on the other side, to be locked into a certain place, unable to leave, to be left with the land no one wanted.

As I write this in 2017, borders and walls have become part of the international conversation. Refugees find themselves crossing borders, and perhaps some of them have wandered into the Borderlands, pushed over by those countries who don't welcome them.

Here in Europe, Brexit fills the news. I voted Remain, but at this point, it seems certain that the passport I hold as a European Citizen will be revoked. I won't be able to cross borders as easily as I have done for most of my adult life and the international landscape I value so much is gradually disappearing beneath rampant nationalism.

I haven't chosen to give up being European – that identity is being taken from me.

So perhaps this is, in fact, a political book, a way I can deal with the complicated and unsolvable problems of borders.

There are no answers, but there are always stories.

Places in the book

As usual with my fiction, I have set the story in real places and modeled the Borderland locations on reality too. You can see some of the pictures that inspired the story at Pinterest.com/jfpenn/map-of-shadows.

Bibliography

I read a lot of books as part of my research. Some of them include:

The Mapmakers' World - Marjo T. Nurminen

Maps: Their Untold Stories - Rose Mitchell & Andrew Janes

Collecting Antique Maps: An Introduction to the History of Cartography - Jonathan Potter

Great Maps: The World's Masterpieces Explored and Explained - Jerry Brotton

The Phantom Atlas: The Greatest Myths, Lies and Blunders on Maps - Edward Brooke-Hitching

The Un-Discovered Islands - Malachy Tallack

Tragic Shores: A Memoir of Dark Travel - Thomas H. Cook

Atlas of Cursed Places: A Travel Guide to Dangerous and Frightful Destinations - Olivier Le Carrer

You Are Here: Personal Geographies and Other Maps of the Imagination - Katharine Harmon

MORE BOOKS BY J.F.PENN

Thanks for joining Sienna and the Mapwalker team in *Map of Shadows*. Sign up at www.JFPenn.com/free to be notified of the next book in the series.

* * *

If you like **supernatural thrillers**, check out the **ARKANE** series as Morgan Sierra and Jake Timber solve supernatural mysteries around the world.

Stone of Fire #1
Crypt of Bone #2
Ark of Blood #3
One Day In Budapest #4
Day of the Vikings #5
Gates of Hell #6
One Day in New York #7
Destroyer of Worlds #8
End of Days #9

* * *

If you like **crime thrillers with an edge of the supernatural**, join Detective Jamie Brooke and museum researcher Blake Daniel, in the London crime thriller trilogy:

Desecration #1
Delirium #2
Deviance #3

* * *

If you enjoy **dark fantasy,** check out:

Risen Gods

American Demon Hunters: Sacrifice

A Thousand Fiendish Angels:
Short stories based on Dante's Inferno

More books coming soon.

You can sign up to be notified of new releases, giveaways and pre-release specials - plus, get a free book!

www.JFPenn.com/free

If you loved the book and have a moment to spare, I would really appreciate a short review on the page where you bought the book. Your help in spreading the word is gratefully appreciated and reviews make a huge difference to helping new readers find the series.

Thank you!

ABOUT THE AUTHOR

J.F.Penn is an award-nominated, *New York Times* and *USA Today* bestselling thriller author. Her ARKANE thrillers have been described as 'Dan Brown meets Lara Croft,' and her London Psychic crime thrillers as 'the love child of Stephen King and PD James.'

Joanna has a Master's degree in Theology from the University of Oxford, Mansfield College and a Graduate Diploma in Psychology from the University of Auckland. She lives in Bath, England but previously lived in New Zealand, Australia and London.

She enjoys traveling and many of her journeys inspire her stories. Joanna loves to read, drink gin & tonic, and soak up European culture through art, architecture and food.

* * *

For writers:

Joanna's site, The Creative Penn, helps people write, publish and market their books through articles, audio, video and online courses. Joanna writes non-fiction for authors and is available internationally for speaking events. Joanna also has a popular podcast for writers.

ACKNOWLEDGMENTS

Thanks to my editor, Jen Blood, for her help with the book, and my proofreader, Wendy Janes. Thanks to Jane Dixon-Smith for the cover and interior print design.

Thanks as ever to my readers, and especially the Pennfriends, for the supportive emails and enthusiastic reviews. You keep me writing!